# Nicotine Dreams

By

## Katie Cunningham

"Nicotine Dreams," by Katie Cunningham. ISBN 1-58939-780-0.

Published 2005 by Virtualbookworm.com Publishing Inc., P.O. Box 9949, College Station, TX 77842, US. ©2005, Katie Cunningham. All rights reserved. No part of this publication may be reproduced, stored in a retrieval system, or transmitted in any form or by any means, electronic, mechanical, recording or otherwise, without the prior written permission of Katie Cunningham.

Manufactured in the United States of America.

# Nicotine Dreams
by
Katie Cunningham

If she hadn't been a closet smoker, she probably wouldn't have become a degenerate gambler. After all, she primarily went to the casino to smoke. She calculated the cost to be about $100 an hour playing quarters.

With the price of the cigarettes and the threat of lung cancer and emphysema added in, she could see the cost of smoking was exorbitant. But oh, the pleasure…

She loved being surrounded by other smokers and being waited on by a "cigarette girl." There were ashtrays at every machine except in the miniscule nonsmoking section. She could remember when people smoked everywhere. As a young R.N., she even smoked at the nursing station. But now that smoking has become even less acceptable than cocaine use, smokers have become desperate in their search for acceptance.

Hello, Jackpot Casino.

# Chapter One

For the first time in her life, Kim drove to the casino. She was meeting her friend Liz for lunch to celebrate Kim's 45th birthday, though still a few days away. She was looking forward to this outing as she thought it might be fun to gamble and she knew she could sneak a few cigarettes at the casino. Kim had only gambled once before on a road trip with her parents. They had stopped for a day in Las Vegas; she was twenty-one at the time. At that age, she still smoked unashamedly, even in front of her mother. Her drug of choice was Pall Mall straights. The unfiltered cigarettes often left specks of tobacco on her teeth, which she would savor, tasting the sweet tobacco juice with her tongue. She and her mother had gone to a downtown casino to drink screwdrivers and play penny slots. It was quality mother-daughter time. They both got a little tipsy and they each had a little luck. They returned to their hotel room with mild hangovers and $25.00 in winnings. Today she wouldn't even risk a hangover, as there was no alcohol served at Jackpot Casino. She hoped her luck was still with her, even though two decades had elapsed since that trip to Vegas.

The huge parking lot at the casino was almost full. She parked at the outskirts of the lot and walked what felt like a half-mile to the entrance. She passed row after row of handicapped parking and was surprised to see nearly every space taken. Casino gambling was a fairly new experience for Minnesota. Only recently had casinos begun to flourish on Indian reservations. Kim looked around for some sign that she was now on a reservation, but all she saw was an upscale suburb. Looming ahead was the source of this newfound prosperity; a modern multi-million dollar structure built of granite and funded by stupidity.

Upon entering the casino, she was amazed at the size, activity, and number of people playing at 11 A.M. on a weekday. She wondered what it must be like on a Friday night. There was row after row of slot machines. The center of the casino was filled with felt-covered blackjack tables. Many of the people there were senior citizens. Women seemed to outnumber the men – at least on the slot machines. She felt her pulse quicken with exhilaration, and she hadn't even placed one bet. She could feel the excitement and the danger. She wasn't sure where the sense of danger came from, as the place was clean and bright. The people were certainly not threatening. It was an internal sense of danger, a feeling that she could lose herself here; she could take risks.

She bought a pack of Merits from a cigarette girl and began to scan the enormous room looking for her friend. She finally found Liz perched on a stool in front of a Wild Cherry slot machine. Her hair was in its perpetual topknot and her slender body was relaxed but the expression on her face was tense. Next to her were an overflowing ashtray and a bag of M&M's. The ever-present cigarette was balanced between two peach tipped fingers.

"Want some M&M's?" Liz asked.

Surprisingly, Kim felt no hunger. She, who never turned down chocolate, suddenly found food repugnant. What she wanted was a cigarette, a Diet Coke, and to play some games.

"I brought fifty bucks," Kim said, "do you think that'll be enough?"

"Only if you're lucky," Liz answered.

Lucky she wasn't, and she soon found herself at the ATM, the first visit of hundreds she would make over the next few years. In time she would come to think of the poker and slot machines as "her" machines. This ATM was also her machine. It was the one Kim usually used, and unlike most of the casino machines, this one was kind to her. She put a card in and money came out. If only she had confined herself to this machine - its odds were very good. She counted her money; $200. She counted her cigarettes; three left. She had bought a pack only two hours ago. She had better start pacing herself, Kim thought. She stopped at the smoke shop on her way back to the slot machines.

"I had to get more money," Kim said when she got back to Liz.

"Maybe you should play something else," Liz advised.

She followed her friend's advice and roamed the casino in search of a "winning" game. She spotted a bank of video poker machines and decided to them a try. Kim sat down, read the flashing message, "Play Five Coins," and obediently dropped five quarters into the slot. She won a few hands and lost a few hands. In one round she had a full house that paid 7 to 1, which really excited her. Then it happened. She was dealt an Ace, Jack and King of Clubs, along with two small

Hearts. She held the clubs and hit the "draw" button". On the re-deal, she received the Ten and Queen of Clubs. Her machine began to sing. She had played poker in the past with friends and she knew the rules. She had a Royal Flush. People began crowding around and congratulating her.

"How much have I won?" she asked, and almost fainted when told $1000.

After being paid nine crisp $100 bills and five twenties, Kim's fate was sealed. It was an expensive win for an addict was born and a life was to be destroyed. She forever blamed that win for her subsequent downfall. Although it is probable that she would have continued to gamble, even if she hadn't won that day, for she loved the casino, the excitement, the games, and the freedom to smoke.

# Chapter Two

Driving home, Kim couldn't keep the smile off her face. She wanted to show Peter the money. Last night they had argued. He hadn't wanted her to go to the casino, because it was a waste of time and money. "Time and money, his two sacred cows," she thought. According to her husband, time should be spent working and money should be hoarded. She didn't believe he was good at handling either of these things. Last week he had gone grocery shopping and had purchased a jar of olives. He always did the shopping because, as he told Kim repeatedly, she was a spendthrift. When he got home from the store, he scoured the receipt in case there were errors – hopefully, in his favor. This time he discovered he had paid a sales tax on the olives even though they were a food item. He spent the next hour ransacking his office, looking for his lists of items that are subject to sales tax. It turned out that olives were exempt. He insisted that Kim drive nine miles to the grocery store with the sales tax information, the receipt and the olives. He wanted his tax refunded, and if they refused, Kim was to return the olives and buy them elsewhere. He also wanted a new receipt so he could be sure she didn't just pay the thirteen cents out of her own pocket.

Kim explained the situation to the gum-cracking teenager who manned the customer service desk at the grocery store. The girl looked at the receipt, then looked at the olives. She cracked her gum, shrugged her shoulders, and said "I'll have to call the manager." The manager repeated the teenager's actions (minus the gum cracking). "Well, I don't know," He said. "Maybe olives are considered a luxury item?" Kim took out Peter's documentation. The manager studied it, then opened the cash register and gave her the thirteen cents. "I also need a new receipt," Kim said with a sheepish smile. She thought it was crazy that this was what her husband considered good time and money management.

Peter was a tyrant who kept her on a short leash. Last night when he said she couldn't go to the casino because she needed to stay home and weed her garden, Kim stood up to him. She told Peter that she had made these plans two weeks ago and that Liz was taking her out to lunch for her birthday. She also said that she was afraid of the garden and wanted him to till it under.

He looked at her, and asked, "You're afraid of the garden?"

"I'm afraid of the snakes in the garden."

"Garter snakes can't hurt you," he said.

"A heart attack would hurt," she replied.

"You're not going to have a heart attack. You hardly ever see a snake out there."

"I see them regularly," she answered, "and I hear them all the time."

"You hear snakes? And what do the snakes say?"

"They don't 'say' anything. They slither," she said, "I hear them slither."

"You hear them slither?"

6

"Quit repeating everything I say!"

"You're making no sense, you can't hear a snake and you can't hear a slither," he said.

"I hear the sound of grass when the snakes slither over it."

"You're hearing the wind blow through the grass."

"I don't care what I'm hearing," she said. "I believe I'm hearing snakes and I'm afraid of snakes and I don't think you should tell me to do something that frightens me!"

"Another thing," he said, changing the subject. "I need handkerchiefs ironed."

Handkerchiefs - another sore spot in her marriage. In this time of Kleenex and Puffs, he was always telling her to iron handkerchiefs. He must blow his nose ten times a day and always use a clean one just to spite her. Once when she returned home from work after midnight, she found a chair blocking access to her bathroom. On it was a note that said "iron handkerchiefs." That meant that she had to go down to the basement in the middle of the night. The basement terrified her even in daylight. There were mice down there, and this was no figment of her imagination. Mouse droppings were everywhere. That night, she flicked the lights on and off several times and called down the stairs repeatedly, yelling, "I'm coming down!" She then proceeded to iron five handkerchiefs, keeping her eyes riveted to the ironing board to avoid seeing any mouse that might decide to scurry across the floor. Her anger that night was palpable. Why couldn't he do his own ironing? After all, she worked, took care of the house, and cooked the meals. It seemed the division of labor was quite unfair. She made no demands of him, and yet he felt entitled to constantly give her orders. But follow his orders she did, for the choice was to do as told or face his rage, and she was a woman who hated conflict.

The night of her first casino win, however, was a very pleasant evening for both of them. She had made a nice dinner and decorated the table with hundred dollar bills. One was propped between the salt and pepper shakers, and two others were folded in fan shapes and placed beneath the silverware. The remaining bills peeked out from under the serving platter in an attractive shell pattern.

He noticed the money as they sat down to eat.

"What's this?"

"I won," she said proudly, as if she had demonstrated some amazing skill that day..

"How much?"

"A thousand bucks," she answered.

Next week when she told him she was going to the casino, he didn't bat an eye.

# Chapter Three

Kim and Peter were complete opposites. She was an extrovert where he was an introvert. She was abstract and he was concrete. She was ruled by her emotions and he by his intellect. She was a nurse and he was an engineer. But despite their differences, their marriage lasted, held together by the glue that often binds two people: children, habit, and the fear of being alone. She was dependent on him financially. They had met in college. He was a morose, compulsive young man. She was sure he would relax and begin to enjoy life once they were married. In the early years, she worked while he went to graduate school. Their two children were the center of her life. Even though her husband never became the fun loving mate she longed for, the children were enough to meet her emotional needs. Once his grad school was over, her husband took a high paying job in the defense industry. He encouraged her to quit her job so she could stay home and take care of him and the kids. She was happy to comply, and the next few years were the happiest of her life. True, there were frequent arguments, where he seemed to think that since she "didn't work," she had unlimited time to perform the various tasks he would assign her. They also argued about money. He was extremely frugal, while she longed for a few luxuries in her life. He felt she spent too much at the grocery store. He complained when she purchased 'convenience foods.' "You're home all day," he said, "you should be able to make things from scratch."

He also thought she spent too much on clothes for the kids.

"They don't need designer brands," he'd say. "Paying sixty bucks for a pair of tennis shoes is shameful."

Kim had an obsession for purses, and her closet was filled Coach's, Dooney's, and Gucci's. Peter had not paid for the purses - she knew better than to charge such items to his account. Instead, she had bought them with the money she received from her parents at Christmas and on her birthday. Even then he saw them as a waste of ever-precious money. When their children went away to college, their marriage became even more strained. She now had free time and longed for a little money to enjoy it. They lived in an affluent neighborhood, and none of her friends or neighbors needed to scrimp as she did. Her husband had frequent business trips, the children were gone, and she was bored, so she decided to return to work. At first her husband resisted the idea, but when she told him she wanted to work in order to save money and build a retirement nest egg, he acquiesced. She did want to work in order to save money. She had always been envious of her husband's investments. The stock market interested her. She often watched CNBC, and making money in the market seemed easy. Her husband had investments and was doing quite well financially, but it was always considered "his" money. She wanted money of her own.

It had been eighteen years since she had worked as a nurse. She had kept her license current by taking the required CEU's and paying the biannual fee. Yet continuing education was not enough to make her feel comfortable applying for a job. She took an intense two-week refresher course, but when it was over she still felt completely inadequate.

"I can't do it," she told her husband at the end of the two weeks. "Nursing has changed too much. I'd be afraid to even try."

Her husband, who had shelled out $265 for the class, was annoyed.

"Look," he said, "at least give it a try. If it's too much, you can always quit."

The nursing shortage in Minneapolis was acute, so even a rusty nurse like her was welcomed in Human Resources. In the application she was to indicate which nursing area she preferred. She thought of all the high tech equipment on the med-surg floors, and of the patients who were hanging on to life by a thread. The responsibility of their well being was terrifying, so she placed a check in the box next to "psychiatry" and prayed that being from a dysfunctional family would be adequate training. One week later, she began her new job.

She loved the job and her patients. She felt strangely comfortable surrounded by psychosis, mania and depression. She was treated with respect and appreciation by the people there, which was a new experience for her. With her first paycheck, she bought a lovely Coach purse: a black bucket bag with heavy brass buckles which attached the strap to the body of the purse.

"I thought you were going to save the money you earn," her husband barked when she showed him her new bag. "You've turned our lives upside down for a new purse!"

"This was my first check, I thought I should treat myself," she answered. "I'll begin saving next week."

And save she did, beginning with her next paycheck. She started a 401K, opened her own checking and savings accounts, and investigated brokerage firms. Even more than handbags, she wanted financial security. She no longer wanted to be dependent on her husband.

As her savings account grew, she ventured into the stock market. She began with small purchases of large, solid companies such as General Electric and Johnson&Johnson. These companies did well, and her confidence grew. Soon she began buying more speculative companies in the technology arena. It was a boom time for tech stocks, which was reflected in her portfolio. For three years she saved and invested her all of her paychecks. Her net worth grew nicely. Her investments, excluding her retirement savings, totaled $42,000 the day she first went to the casino. Gambling would soon put an end to her investing.

Kim was chronically tired from working day-night rotations at work. She often had difficulty with daytime sleeping. Plus, she still had the same responsibilities at home. She constantly felt overwhelmed. She opted for a permanent evening schedule; she would work from three in the afternoon and be home by midnight.

"Who's going to cook my dinner?" her husband bellowed when she told him the news. "I should never have allowed you to go back to work."

He complained incessantly. She tried leaving dinner in the crock-pot, but this didn't satisfy him as he wanted someone to wait on him. When a weekend contract became available, she took it. This meant she would be working twelve hours every Saturday and

Sunday, but be off Monday through Friday. In exchange for working long hours every weekend, she was treated with pay and benefits that full-time employees received. "Perfect," she thought. She'd be at work or asleep all weekend when he was home, and during the week, when he went to work and traveled, she'd be home. She could still make his dinner every night. Work on the weekend meant they would eat late, but Peter liked that. He said it felt European. He was satisfied with this new schedule, and the battles at home ceased. They settled into their normal cold war. She had been working the weekend schedule for six months when Liz called and invited her to the casino.

# Chapter Four

Her next trip to the casino was with her friend, Pat. They were both excited on the drive to the casino. The drive was endless because Pat thought she knew a shortcut and the thirty-one mile drive became forty-five miles.

If in Italy all roads lead to Rome, it seemed true that in Minneapolis all roads led to the Jackpot Casino. Eventually they arrived. Their adrenalin was so pumped up, they almost ran a quarter mile from their parking space to the door. Kim had suggested that Pat drop her off at the door, but Pat refused.

"What kind of a friend are you anyway, expecting me to walk all the way from the parking lot alone?"

Their bickering stopped as they entered the casino. Kim could see that the place had the same effect on Pat that it had on her. Pat looked transfixed and stood there like a deer blinded by headlights.

Suddenly Pat came back to life, "Where are the ATM's?" she asked. "I've got to get some money!" She took out forty dollars and said "This is all I'm going to spend."

Pat's bank allowed her to withdraw a maximum of $200 a day. She ended up making five $40 withdraw-

14

als. She was all over the casino trying nickel and quarter slots. She played a little video poker, and boldly slipped a twenty into a dollar "red, white and blue," but got nothing. She went back to quarters, and then switched back to the "red, white and blue" machines. She got three sevens in the proper colors, which came to a $165 win. She was ecstatic. She found Kim, who had never left the machine that had given her the royal the preceding week.

"Look," Pat exclaimed, holding up her bucket of quarters, "I won!"

In reality, she was down thirty-five dollars, but what the heck! In her heart she was a winner.

"Good for you. I'm not having any luck at all. My machine is really tight," Kim said.

"Tight?" Pat asked.

"Yeah, when they pay they're loose and when they don't pay, they're tight. That's the jargon," Kim said.

Suddenly Kim's machine "loosened" up. She was dealt three aces and got a fourth on the draw. She was playing bonus poker, and four aces paid one hundred dollars. This allowed her to continue playing for a while. One hour later, they were both broke.

"Well, that was dumb." Pat said. "We should have quit when we had won some of our money back."

"Yeah, but I hate to lose anything. I wanted to win it all back," Kim said.

They agreed to not return to the casino, as they had learned their lesson.

The next week both of their husbands were out of town on Monday and Tuesday. The men called home nightly when out of town, so the women decided to go to the casino after the Monday night calls. They would be able to stay as late as they liked and never even have to tell their husbands they had gone. Neither husband was pleased with their last casino trip, even though Pat and Kim had minimized their losses. They knew their husbands would be furious if they found out they had each lost $200. Their Monday night plan was to win that money back.

"We have to play smarter," Kim said. "Every time we double our money in a machine, we take it out. We don't just play till it's gone."

Unfortunately, they rarely doubled their money, and when they did, they didn't want to upset the rhythm of the machine by taking their money out.

By midnight they had both spent the $200 they had been able to get from the ATM's. It was time to head home, and they were not happy about it. They ransacked their purses for every last bit of change. The linty quarters from the bottoms of their handbags were dropped into slot machines. Two rumpled dollar bills were traded in for a roll of nickels. These two women, who shouldn't have a financial care in the world, were desperate for money. They wanted to win back what they had lost, and they did not want to go home.

"I can't go home yet," Kim cried at the end of the night. "I still have cigarettes left."

They decided to try the ATM's one more time, in case some computer glitch had occurred and the machines would not realize they were at their daily limit. They each went to a machine, slid in their debit cards and they punched in their PINs. They pushed the button next to "withdrawal" and coded in $200. Ten crisp twenties slid into each of their drawers. Pat and Kim stared at the money, confused.

"The day must start at midnight," Kim said. "It's a new day to the ATM."

They made many trips to the smoke shop for cigarettes and painkillers that night. Their heads ached from smoking so much and eating so little. Kim's stomach also hurt from the assortment of pills she had taken, but an antacid solved that problem. They were two middle-aged women sneaking around behind their husbands' backs. They were smoking and gambling and staying up all night. They didn't eat and were unable to pull themselves away from their machines to go to the bathroom until practically wetting their pants. They had never had so much fun in their lives. They played until morning and drove home during rush hour. Guilt set in during the tedious drive. They vowed to quit gambling right now.

"We've each lost $600 in less than a week," Pat said.

"Well, I'm still up," Kim said, "I won a thousand, remember."

"I don't care, I'm not gambling anymore. It's stupid," Pat said. And from the stern expression on her face, it was obvious that she meant it.

They each went home to their respective houses where they napped and tried to put the casino out of their minds. When their husbands called home on Tuesday night, neither woman mentioned their Monday night visit to the casino.

At midnight Kim's phone rang.

"We can get more money from the ATM now," Pat said.

"I thought you were never going there again," Kim said.

Pat answered, "I have to win that money back. It's my household money for the month."

Twenty minutes later they were on their way. Kim drove. They found a parking spot near the door. This was a first and "a good sign," Pat predicted.

"So much for good signs," Kim groused two hours and two hundred dollars later.

"I have twenty bucks left," Pat said, "And I feel lucky."

She slid her last twenty into a "double diamond" slot machine. She was down to her last six credits when three diamonds lined up in a perfect row in the center of the screen. The machine made an incredible racket and the progressive jackpot lights above the bank of machines began flashing "winner." Pat had just won $800. It took about half an hour and five employees for her to get her money. Pat was paid with seven hundred dollar bills and five twenties.

"How come all the twenties?" she asked Kim.

"I don't know - maybe so you'll tip. Maybe so you'll keep playing."

"Well, I'm done playing." Pat said, tucking the hundred dollar bills into the zipper compartment of her Paloma Picasso purse. "With your thousand dollar win and my $800, we're pretty much even with this place. I think we should get the hell out of here."

The two didn't get far. They decided they would not touch the seven one hundred dollar bills. Pat lent Kim fifty dollars to see if they could win a little more before heading home. The $800 lasted until 3 P.M., at which time they found themselves broke and exhausted. Their husbands were due home in a few hours, so they had no choice but to leave the casino. Once home, Kim rushed around the house - cleaning, ironing, preparing dinner – and by the time her husband got home, everything was in order. He asked what she had been doing the last two days.

"Nothing special," Kim answered. "Cleaning, reading, rented a video, just the normal stuff."

She went to bed early, but was unable to sleep. The thousand dollars she had won was gone and she owed Pat $400. She had started to worry about money, but despite this she longed to return to the casino.

# Chapter 5

During the following year, Kim developed a pattern. Her husband would leave for work in the morning; she would leave fifteen minutes later and head to the casino. At first, she limited herself to her $200 a day from the ATM, but soon she began writing checks. Initially she limited herself to a $200 a day check writing privilege, but that was quickly raised to $1000. Between the checks and the ATM withdrawals, she was now able to get her hands on $1200 every time she visited the casino. She also had a $5000 ready reserve limit on her checking account. In no time, Kim was $5000 in debt. She had never owed money before and had always paid cash for the things she would buy. Her debt weighed heavily on her. The interest rate on the ready reserve was sixteen percent, so even if she used her entire paycheck to pay down this loan, it would to take a long time to fully repay. She worried nonstop that her husband would open her bank statement and see the loan. She was a wreck on Saturdays when she had to work and Peter would be taking in the mail, afraid that he would see all the money she owed. She decided she had to sell a stock and pay off the ready reserve. Then she could then start over, quit gambling, and start saving her money again.

Her husband never did open her mail. She kept all her records in a personal file cabinet, which he never touched. His only access to her finances was the computer where she methodically kept an online record of her investments. Daily he would check her portfolio to see her current net worth. Her investments were still growing nicely.

During the three years she had worked and saved, (prior to the time she had started gambling), she had accumulated a portfolio of five stocks: GE, Johnson&Johnson, Intel, Sun Microsystems, and Cisco. All were doing very well, especially the tech stocks. She told her husband that since technology seemed to be the fastest growing area, she was going to sell Johnson&Johnson to buy more aggressive companies. She had to tell him if she was going to sell something, since she had gains and knew this would be a taxable event. Peter was a great believer in the "buy and hold" method of investing and felt it was a mistake to sell anything, but she assured him that she could make more elsewhere, so he agreed as long as she paid the taxes on her capital gains. She sold JNJ. She would now have enough to pay off her loan and give Peter money for the IRS. She slept well the night her loan was paid off.

"So, what are you going to buy now?" he asked her one evening at dinner.

She hadn't worked that part out yet. She had to have someplace where she could tell him she had invested the money. The next day she investigated stocks online. She saw that Internet stocks were increasing rapidly in value despite the fact that they were all losing money. Kim knew eventually these stocks would collapse and be worth nothing, so she picked out two especially overpriced stocks and added them to her online portfolio without actually purchasing them. She was sure in time they would be worthless and her husband would have the enjoyment of saying "I told you so."

She hadn't gone to the casino or smoked a cigarette for a week. She had been smoking a lot while gambling and found herself extremely nervous as she went through nicotine withdrawal. At work that weekend she talked one of the doctors into giving her a prescription for Nicorette gum. She loved the gum and found it almost as satisfying as smoking. Soon she was chewing fifteen to twenty pieces a day. The gum was expensive, but the prescriptions were easy to come by. As a nurse, she knew a lot of doctors who were willing to write prescriptions to help her quit smoking. She continued to think of the casino, wishing there was a gum that would take away that desire. She bought a hand held video poker machine which she played whenever possible. It didn't take away her desire to play, but made her want to return to the casino even more.

Her gambling hiatus lasted two weeks. Her husband went on a three-day business trip. With him gone it seemed the casino was calling her name, and she could not resist. Kim decided to take her ATM card, but leave her checkbook at home. In theory she couldn't get into too much trouble that way. The $200 was gone in less than two hours, so Kim drove the thirty-one miles home, got her checkbook, and drove another thirty-one miles back to the casino. She wrote $1000 in checks that night and lost it all. Once again, she was into her ready reserve. She drove home again, went into her husband's money stash and took out $200. She again returned to the casino, but won nothing. She drove home again, tired and with her head aching, but returned to the casino with a credit card. She didn't know the PIN number for the card so she couldn't use the ATM. Instead, she slid the card through a credit card machine hooked up to the main cashier's cage. The fees for cash advances were incredible but she didn't hesitate. She accepted the fee and proceeded to the counter. She withdrew $1000, and this time she didn't bother with twenties.

"I'd like it in large bills," she told the cashier, who handed her ten one hundred dollar bills.

Kim had decided that her only hope for winning her money back was to increase her bets. She didn't even pause at the quarter video poker machines that had been devouring her money all night. She went straight to the one-dollar double bonus poker machines. She played the max, five dollars per hand. She estimated her play at 600 hands per hour, which meant she was running $3000 an hour through the machines.

Soon an employee asked her if she'd like a player's card. "You can get money back - earn free meals, rooms, shows. It doesn't cost you anything," he said.

"No thanks. I don't plan to come here again," she told him.

He smiled disbelievingly. Kim caught the look. "Who do these people think they are," she thought angrily.

She didn't return home for three days. She left messages daily on her husband's voicemail at work, telling him that she'd be out that evening and would not be home to take his call. She assured him everything was fine at home and that she was spending her evenings with friends, going out to dinner and movies. The casino upped her check-writing limit to $2000. She continued to write checks and use the ATM. When her daily limit on all advances was reached, she would leave the casino and drive to her bank in order to cash checks against her ready reserve. At the end of the three days, she was tapped out, unable to get her hands on any more money. She had lost over $12,000 on credit cards and ready reserve, enough to pay for a small car. When her husband returned home from his trip, she told him she had sold GE and bought more Internet stocks. She had now been gambling for one year. Her forty-sixth birthday was rapidly approaching.

# Chapter Six

Her husband, of course, was aware that Kim gambled. He wasn't as smart as he thought he was, but he wasn't stupid either. He did not, however, have any idea of the extent of her gambling and therefore was quite surprised when Kim mentioned one evening that she was joining Gamblers Anonymous.

"You haven't gambled enough to join any group," he said.

"Well," Kim said, not wanting to divulge too much information because she still lived in fear of his discovering all the money she'd lost. "I may not gamble that much, but I think about it all the time and it's a problem for me. I'm afraid if I don't get help, I will develop a gambling problem."

Her husband continued to grumble, but Kim felt good. She was finally going to get help. She figured she'd meet people in the group who had lost everything, and that would scare her into giving up gambling. She could learn from them and avoid their mistakes. The following Monday, after an early dinner, she put on her coat and grabbed her purse – a vintage Gucci, and rushed out the door, afraid she'd be late.

"The meeting's at eight," she called to Peter as she was leaving. "I'll be home as soon as it's over."

Her husband muttered something about twelve steps and lack of self-control as she entered the garage. She felt so hopeful on the drive, as if walking into the room would solve her gambling problem as easily as Nicorette kept her from smoking. She longed for stories of ruin and of people turning to crime and bankruptcy. The first person in the meeting to speak was a dumpy woman about Kim's age.

"My husband and I are getting a divorce because of my gambling," she sobbed. "He found an ATM receipt from the casino. He demanded my checking account statements for the last year. I thought he would kill me. I've lost almost $1000 in the last year," she wailed, "My life is ruined."

"A thousand bucks," Kim thought, "that's nothing. That isn't even twenty dollars a week. What kinds of lightweights were at this meeting?" The time in the meeting dragged. There seemed to be a lot of ceremonial reading of rules and steps. Kim, who had been on an adrenaline high since her first trip to the casino, found this boring. She had stayed out of the casino all week and hoped that in time GA would prove helpful. The following week she attended her second meeting. She dreaded going because it was cold out and she was sure she'd once again be bored to death. And she was. The meeting seemed endless. A rather unpleasant side of Kim appeared during this meeting. She found herself looking down on these people, seeing them as lowlifes and losers. She had nothing in common with them. She could hardly wait to get out of the room; she was embarrassed to be there.

The following Monday, she told her husband she would be late returning from GA.

"They all go out after the meeting, that's the best part," she told him. "That's when they really talk and spill their guts. That's where the real healing takes place."

"Oh, for God's sake," her husband groaned, "you don't need healing!"

"Anyway, I'll be late," Kim said. "I'll be at Perkins or someplace. Don't wait up." (As if he would, she thought to herself).

She went upstairs, retrieved her checkbook and ATM card, and flew out the door. She never even glanced at the freeway exit she should take to go to her meeting – she was on her way to the casino.

Once there, she pulled up a chair next to a middle-aged man wearing a shiny mask over his face. At first she didn't notice the mask, as the casino was dimly lit. She just thought he had shiny, taut skin. He smiled broadly as she sat down as if happy to see her.

"Hi," he said, "have a seat! I have a feeling these machines are gong to hit soon."

"Great!" she answered. "Have you been here long?"

"Since August," he answered. "Not just at theses machines. I play all over, mainly nickels and some quarters. I've been at these machines for three hours with nothing. I'm sure they'll hit soon. No one won at the one you're at either."

Kim counted the months on her fingers.

"You've been here five months," she said. "How can you afford it?"

"Insurance settlement," he said, pointing to his face.

"Burns," she thought. "Those are burns under that shiny clear mask."

"And comps," he said. "They've been giving me a free room since August and I'm giving them my insurance settlement. I'm on a strict budget, $200 a day. For that I've been getting a free room and a free buffet everyday. Of course, I had quite a few comps coming before my accident. If I hadn't had those, I don't know if my play would be enough for a free room. Also, I have the casino hold my money, so they know I have a lot left. That may motivate them to keep me living here."

"You actually live here," Kim asked. "You have nowhere else to go?"

"No," he answered, "I gave up my apartment and sold all my belongings except for clothes and toiletries. I took the cash and checked in here. I have enough to live here fourteen more years - if I stick to my budget."

Kim rapidly calculated that he must have a million dollars tucked away in the casino vault.

"Have you thought of investing that money?" she asked. "It would really grow and your future could be quite secure."

"I'd be afraid of losing it if I put it in the stock market," he said.

"You're losing it at these machines," Kim said.

"But I'm losing it doing what I love," he said. "How many people can spend the last fourteen years of their lives doing exactly what they want? All I want to do is gamble, smoke, eat one good meal a day, and visit with other gamblers. I can afford to do that for years so I consider myself very lucky."

"But you're still a young man," Kim said. "What will you do when your money runs out?"

"I have many health problems," he confided. "It's doubtful I'll live even fourteen years. That's why it's so important for me to enjoy myself."

His machine did warm up. He lined up three hippos several times and was able to jump for bananas. Once his banana bunch was so huge, the characters in the slot machine formed a conga line and danced for him. He was thrilled.

"If I hadn't won soon," he said, "it would have been time for supper and bed. I always eat and go to bed when the $200 is gone. Budget, you know."

Kim found herself thinking frequently of this man, of his disfigured face, his shortened life expectancy, alone, and with no home other than a casino. She thought of him with envy, and could not imagine a better life than spending every last day you had playing at the casino. She would need a lot more money than he had in order to live out that dream - she could never get by on $200 a day.

She decided it was time to take a different approach to her gambling. She was not like those losers in GA because gambling has destroyed nothing in her life. She and her husband still had plenty of money. They were in no danger. "Moderation is the key," she thought. She had to quit this all or nothing mentality. She would learn to gamble in moderation. Gambling was now to become an enjoyable pastime for her. She would play with a set amount of money, and when it was gone it was gone. She would also start using a Player's Card. She might as well get those free meals and other comps. She would eat when she was at the casino to avoid headaches from going hungry. She would also limit herself to one pack of Carlton's per visit, the weakest cigarettes she could find. She was going to be normal! Once she was normal again, she'd be able to pay off her debts. She'd be a better wife to her husband and spend more time with her adult children. "If only I had grandchildren," she thought. They would fill the void that caused her to gamble.

She was "normal" only until her money and cigarettes ran out. Then she'd hit the cash machine and the smoke shop. She continued to use her Player's Card, but little else about her play changed. She quickly slipped back into her old patterns.

# Chapter Seven

Her respite from compulsive gambling and chronic lying to her husband came on the weekend during which she spent twenty-four hours locked in a psychiatric intensive care unit with ten of the most severely mentally ill and often dangerous people to be found in the city. "It was the blind leading the blind," she often thought as she unlocked the three heavy doors that separated her patients from freedom. She believed herself to be a good nurse. True, her medical skills may have been poor and her paperwork often sloppy, but the important thing was she cared about these people. Staunch Republican that she was, she could still feel their pain. Few nurses liked working this unit. Many were afraid, and others just disliked the intensity found in such severe mental illnesses. Kim rarely felt fear and amazingly was never injured. She treated her patients with respect and affection. She joked with them and gave a lot of meds and hugs. She tucked them into bed, made cocoa, and called them "sweethearts." They often called her "Mom". On this Saturday morning, a paranoid patient approached the nursing station asking for hand lotion. Kim handed him a light blue bottle.

"I can't use that kind," he said. "It's KGB blue."

"Don't be silly, honey," Kim answered. "Anyone can see it's CIA green."

He took the bottle. That was her style, and it usually worked. She often thought her nursing instructors would be appalled – this was not the way nursing was taught in schools.

Despite the double life she lived at home, at work she was open and unable to keep secrets. Her struggles with cigarettes and gambling were well known. It was the job, in fact, that had started her smoking again after twenty years of being nicotine free. Psych patients smoke probably more than any group on Earth. The most important times of the day for her patients were the hours when the smoking room was open. The staff would buy cigarettes and dole them out during the smoke breaks. It had been a long time since Kim had been around smokers, and was surprised at how appealing the cigarettes looked. Even after twenty years, in her heart she was still a smoker. She began purchasing cigarettes for patients, and always carried a pack in her purse. One day she went to lunch with a group of coworkers who smoked. They ate at the bar across the street from the hospital not to drink, but because smoking was permitted. Without thinking, Kim pulled the pack out of her purse and lit up. Her coworkers looked as surprised as Kim felt. The cigarette tasted wonderful. She began smoking on weekends. During the week she was a nonsmoker. Her husband never knew of her weekend vice.

Back in the ICU, she was having a very busy day. She was the only nurse scheduled and had just received her second admission. The patient was filthy and probably hadn't bathed in weeks. She imagined lice in his matted hair and found herself scratching her own scalp. She knew she'd be using Kwell tonight. She always did when she started thinking about cooties. The police had brought in her patient. They found him dumpster diving, and when they attempted to intervene he became agitated and assaulted a policeman. In the squad car, he began to rant about God and Satan. He made little sense and was obviously psychotic, so he was taken to the hospital instead of jail. Because of his assaultive behavior, he was sent to the ICU. He talked to himself nonstop and was constantly moving. Side effects from years of antipsychotic medication were the cause of his tongue flicking in and out of his mouth and his fingers forming nonexistent particles into perfect little balls. He did not look threatening; he was just a lost soul. Kim needed to check in his belongings, so she put on rubber gloves as she did not want to touch his dirty clothing. His ancient camel hair coat was covered with tiny moth eaten holes.

"This coat has seen better days," Kim remarked.

"Yes," he answered. "I've walked through acid rain."

"Yes, I can see that," Kim said, suddenly stripping off her gloves and extending her hands to him. He seemed as confused by the gesture as she was, but he took her hands in his and smiled at her. When she smiled back, her eyes filled with tears. She did not know why.

# Chapter Eight

On Monday mornings she was always exhausted. She would get little sleep on the weekend with her long hours. She was also always keyed up when she got home, and it took her hours for her to settle down. Her work was physical with lots of walking, bending, and sometimes lifting, but it was the emotional aspect of the job that wore her out the most. Her patients lived in waking nightmares which they could not escape, and she could not ignore their suffering.

Once she tried to explain her job to her husband to make him understand the fatigue she felt at the end of her workweek.

"You only work two days a week," he argued. "I work five and I travel a lot, which is really tiring. Some nights I don't get into my hotel till near midnight, and then I have to get up early and go to meetings. It seems to me that you have it made."

"Yes, but your job doesn't make you want to come home some nights and cry yourself to sleep," she answered.

"I have to write proposals for the government," he said. "The government – all that red tape. If that isn't enough to make someone cry, I don't know what is. Anyway, if you are so sick of your job, why don't you find something else? There are certainly more pleasant nursing jobs available. I don't know why you can't get a job at a nice hospital working with people who are really sick."

"Let me tell you, my patients are beyond sick! They're tortured! They've lost everything - their families, their jobs, and their own identities. They don't even have the real world. They live in an alien place where their illness becomes their world. Just because I need to talk about my job, it doesn't mean I'm sick of it. I just want you to understand what I do and give me some credit."

"I'll accept that they're sick," Peter said, "but I don't understand why you want to work with them. It seems you've got some revolving door policy at that hospital. Your patients never get well. They come into the hospital, get a little better, are discharged and then return a few weeks later. The whole system stinks. I think you'd be better off if you worked with people you could cure. A job that made you feel good. Try working with tax paying productive citizens. They need help too."

"I didn't become a nurse to have fun. I became a nurse in order to help people."

"Well, a person needs to have results in order to find a job rewarding. At least at the end of my day I know I've accomplished something. At the end of a project I have something to show for it."

"Bombs, you make bombs," Kim yelled. "That's some accomplishment. Where would we be without them?"

"I'll tell you where we'd be. We'd be speaking Russian, or Japanese, or German. We'd be living in a world of dictators and tyranny! And as for your precious patients, if it weren't for my bombs, they'd be warehoused in some snake pit because that's the way totalitarian governments treat the mentally ill. So just knock off all the holier than thou shit, cause I'm sick of it."

"And I'm sick of fighting with you!" Kim grabbed her purse and headed for the door.

"I suppose you're going to that stupid casino now," he yelled after her, "Hey nurse, heal thyself!"

She ruminated about their argument as she drove to the casino. He would never understand her job. For twenty-three years she'd been listening to him talk about his job, about his stress, but his talks bored her and she tended to tune him out. He stewed about proposals and algorithms. She'd been married to an engineer for half her life and she didn't even know what an algorithm was. She was upset, but she knew that it would pass once she started playing. The gambling was destroying her; it had turned her into a liar and put her in debt. The long hours and smoking were harming her physically, and yet she couldn't stop. The machines were like a drug to her. All conscious thought disappeared and she ceased to worry about anything except getting her hands on more money so she could continue to play. She couldn't rationally explain this compulsion to gamble, this need to obliterate the real world and enter a place where nothing existed but a video poker machine. She sometimes wished she had found this nirvana through cocaine or marijuana use - it would have been so much cheaper.

That night she had very little money available. She was at her limit of $5000 on her ready reserve. Her balance in her checking account was under $100, so she withdrew eighty dollars. Sixty of it was lost to the nickel slots. She found a bank of two-cent "Bee-Zerk" machines and lost her last twenty playing a game called "Ring Em Up." Her bonus pool was over 1000 credits, and Kim was tempted to bounce a check in order to keep playing. But for once, her reason prevailed. A thousand credits on a two-cent machine added up to twenty bucks, while the fee for bouncing a check was twenty-five dollars. She forced herself to go home. She needed to make up with her husband. She needed to pull herself together.

# Chapter Nine

Her husband was sleeping when she got home. Kim decided then to pull her head out of the sand and face her financial dilemma. If she could get a handle on her finances, her anxiety level would decrease dramatically. If she were less stressed, she'd be able to fight the urge to gamble. She was going to turn over a new leaf that moment. She was going to give up the smoking and the gum too. She could do it.

Kim got herself a Diet Coke and an ashtray, went up to the office, opened the window and turned on the fan. It was only twenty degrees outside. Peter would have a fit if he knew she had a window open. She hoped the frigid night air blowing into the room would erase any evidence of her smoking. She lit up. Tonight she'd solve the financial worries; tomorrow she'd quit smoking. She knew she could keep from smoking if she kept chewing Nicorette, but was concerned about the amount of gum she consumed. She was thinking of going on the patch to get off the gum. The gambling was intertwined into the problem of smoking. If she could get herself off nicotine once and for all, her gambling days would be over.

She inhaled deeply and logged onto the Internet. Where should she start? With the good news of her assets, or should she go directly to the debts that were eating a hole in her gut? She decided to start on a positive note and pulled up her portfolio. At first glance it was awesome, it showed nine stocks valued at $137,000. The scary part was that she only owned three of them. The other six were stocks she had only pretended to buy when she had sold other assets to pay for her gambling losses. The six nonexistent stocks had quadrupled in value since her imaginary purchases. They were so overvalued that she was sure they had to crash soon. Kim wondered if she was becoming religious from praying all the time. At the casino she prayed for luck, and at home she prayed for a bear market. The stocks she actually owned had a net worth of $47,000. She deleted them from her portfolio. She spent a couple of hours researching investments until she found a few stocks that seemed highly overvalued. She added $47,000 worth of Amazon, eBay, and E Toys to her entirely fictional portfolio. "Crash baby, crash," she thought, then clicked into her Charles Schwab account. She placed market orders to sell her entire portfolio. Within days she would have approximately $47,000 in her money market. "Not too bad," she thought, "that will be more than enough to cover my debts."

The following week she diligently paid off every cent she owed. She sent $5000 to her bank to cover the ready reserve. She paid off the $16,000 she owed on three VISA cards, and the $17000 she owed Master-Card. She was out of debt and still had $9000 left over. Six thousand of this she would have to give to Peter to cover the taxes on the capital gains. This left $3000, which she transferred into her checking account. She now had a cushion, so even if she made a mistake in her checking account, she would not go into ready reserve. She felt good.

The following weekend she hit up one of the docs at work for a prescription for Nicotine patches. He commended her on her desire to quit smoking and wrote out a lengthy prescription of decreasing doses.

"This should do it," he said. "I tapered the doses; you shouldn't feel any withdrawal at all."

She did not know that nicotine products would be available over the counter before her prescription ran out.

Work was abuzz that weekend with gossip. One of the nurses, Sandy, was on a medical leave. She had stolen a credit card and driver's license from a co-worker and used them to get a $1000 cash advance at the casino. No one could believe it – everyone loved Sandy! She was one of the best nurses, hard working and compassionate. Their boss had sprung into action, pulled some strings, and got her into inpatient treat-ment for gambling addiction. No one had even guessed she had a problem. Kim had run into her occasionally at the casino, so she knew Sandy gambled. Rumors ran rampant that charges would be filed, she might go to jail, she might be fired, or she might lose her nursing license! Who knew what punishments lay in store for poor Sandy?

"She should have stolen my credit card," Kim told a coworker. "I would have understood her problem. I wouldn't even have reported her. She could have just paid me back."

"She probably figured your cards were charged to their limits. Let's face it, you seem to have a bigger problem than she has," the coworker replied.

Kim was stung. "Well, I'm not in treatment, I'm not in jail and I've never broken any laws. I don't owe one cent to anyone and probably have more in my checking account than your do," Kim replied. And thanks to selling everything she owned last week, she was speaking the truth.

"Sorry," her coworker said, "It's just that you talk about gambling a lot more than Sandy ever did. I guess I always thought you had the problem not her. I suppose if you really have a problem, you learn to keep it under wraps."

The incident with Sandy had shaken Kim. There was suddenly a lot of talk on the unit about gambling addiction. Money had been stolen from staff and patients alike – Sandy became a prime suspect. "I had better keep quiet about my own gambling," Kim thought. She didn't want her coworkers to think she had a problem like Sandy's. The secrecy felt like a huge weight on her. She'd have to be careful of what she said both at work and at home. She could only be honest from now on with her closest friends, and she could only talk to them because they were fighting their own battles with the casino. She made it clear to everyone that she worked with that she had kicked her bad habits. Kim told them that she was a new woman that she no longer smoked or gambled. And in her heart, she did mean what she told them.

"Keep busy," she told herself. Peter had no trips planned this week, which was good. Gambling was especially appealing when she could go out late at night and stay till morning. She loved the casino during the wee hours when could always get on her favorite machines and never had worry about sitting next to a nonsmoker who would cough and carry on because of Kim's smoke. At 3 A.M. in a casino, everyone smoked. She made plans for every day that week. On two of days, she would meet her kids at their jobs and have lunch with them. Another day she would take her mother shopping. The fourth day that week, she planned to have her carpets shampooed and had to stay home. Kim was on the road to recovery, and she would not become another Sandy. She left her cigarettes at work that weekend for the patients. She chewed her last three pieces of Nicorette gum on the drive home. She had gotten her patch prescription filled at work and now dutifully peeled the backing off a piece and placed it on her upper arm. It itched terribly.

When she went to bed, she was awakened by wild, sexual dreams. She had no idea such a deranged pervert dwelled deep within her id. "God," Kim thought. "I've given up gambling and smoking, now I'm into pornography. What kind of person am I?" The following night the dreams occurred again. "It must be the patch," she thought. She got up to read the directions. She was to leave it on for twenty-four hours then replace it. She figured, like most medication side effects, this would decrease in time. She went back to bed and spent the next six hours basking in erotica. By the third night, she could hardly wait to go to bed, which worried her. "I'm turning into one sick puppy," she thought.

However, just as she was developing a taste for this creative sexuality, the dreams changed. They were no longer sexual, but frightening. She woke up and ripped off the patch. From then on, she put a patch on in the morning and took it off before bed. It worked just as well that way.

She developed puffy red rectangles wherever she wore a patch. They lingered there for days after the patch was removed. Kim didn't want her husband to see this checkerboard; he'd think she had some weird, communicable disease. She couldn't tell him Nicotine patches caused them, because he still didn't know she smoked. She started wearing them on her rump, a place her husband hadn't looked for years. She was concerned about these raised, red marks. They must be some sort of allergic reaction, she figured. Kim certainly didn't want to go into anaphylactic shock. She studied her naked rear end in the mirror, noting that chess could now be played on her backside.

# Chapter Ten

She did not gamble or smoke for several weeks. She continued to wear her patches and was rapidly running out of unblemished skin. The patches helped the nicotine jitters, but didn't satisfy the oral gratification she received from cigarettes and Nicorette gum. She filled that void with chocolate. More skin was created on which to stick patches. She thought she would be happy if she quit going to the casino, but she wasn't. Kim was bored and miserable. Her moods were becoming as erratic as her periods. She cried frequently and was always irritable. She couldn't sleep; she was hot all the time. These weren't the hot flashes she had come to expect from her menopausal friends. This was one hot flash that began at age forty-six and continued to age forty-nine, when she finally began hormone replacement. Kim found herself unable to pass a thermostat without turning it down. Her coworkers began wearing wool sweaters and her husband donned long johns. Coffee could only be consumed on frigid winter mornings when she could drink it on the deck while wearing only a nightgown. To drink coffee in a warm room was unthinkable, as the caffeine increased her already overheated system to the boiling point. Sleep was elusive. It took her hours to dose off only to be awakened by night sweats. By morning, all of the covers were invariably on the floor. Her bedroom faced east, and the morning sun burned through the blinds and turned the room into an oven. One morning at breakfast, her husband ruminated about his risk for prostate cancer.

"It's not fair," he said. "If a man lives long enough, he will eventually get prostate cancer. The only thing women get is breast cancer, and that's only a small percentage of them."

Kim longed to put rat poison in his oatmeal.

If quitting gambling and smoking was difficult by itself, with menopause it became impossible. Kim had changed during the last couple years, perhaps because of the stress she felt from her gambling addiction. Perhaps it was a result of the increased confidence she had gained from her job. Or perhaps it was simply menopausal irritability. Whatever the cause, she no longer felt the need to acquiesce to her husband's many demands. She began to view him as a tyrant and a compulsive, cold fish. He was so set in his ways; everything had to be done according to his rules of life. They began to argue constantly. The first major fight began at dinner one night, when Kim had made a casserole.

Her husband glared at the large dish she placed on the table.

"What's that?" he snapped.

"It's a casserole," she answered.

"Does it have soup in it?"

"Cream of Chicken," was her reply.

"I don't eat casseroles, especially if they're made with soup. I ate tuna fish casserole every Friday from birth till graduating from college. I've told you, I will never eat a casserole again."

"It doesn't have any tuna fish in it."

"It's still a casserole, I won't eat it."

"You haven't even tried it. It's good. It was my favorite when I was growing up. My mother used to make it."

"I don't eat casseroles."

"Listen, for twenty-four years we have only eaten what you want. Tonight I want casserole, and I think it's my turn to choose our dinner. I'm not just some servant who cooks what you want. I have preferences too."

"If you want something special to eat, you should cook it for yourself and bring it to work on Saturday and Sunday. You shouldn't expect me to have to eat it. Plus, think of the money you'd save if you brought your lunch instead of eating out. You waste so much money at restaurants, I have always brought my lunch, that's how I've managed to save so much."

"I cook five nights a week and on the weekends I work twelve hours a day. I'll be damned if I'm going to cook those days too. Anyway, I enjoy going out to eat. Maybe we'd have a better marriage if you had saved less and we went out more."

"Now you're saying we have something wrong with our marriage," he yelled.

"You probably think our marriage is fine, because you're selfish and everything is done your way. I'm sick of it. This casserole symbolizes our marriage. I can't have it because you don't want it. I can't eat watermelon for breakfast because you think that's a lunch food. We can't have cantaloupe for lunch because it's a breakfast food. We can't have sandwiches or omelets for dinner, because they're lunch and breakfast foods. Give me a break! I'm sick of all your rules, and if I want to eat a goddamn BLT for dinner I should be able to!"

"You are getting a smart mouth, and it's not very attractive," he told her. "You need to apologize, and then I want you to freeze that casserole so you can bring it to work for your lunches. Now, fix me something suitable for dinner. I want salmon, asparagus and some fried potatoes with onion in them."

"I will no longer be your slave," was her parting comment to him as she headed for her car. She needed a cigarette and Jackpot Casino was beckoning her.

As she walked from the smoke shop to the gaming area, she remembered she was still wearing a patch. She slid her hands down her pants, hoping no one would notice her peeling it off. It took a bit of tugging to remove, and she did receive a couple of disgusted looks, but she didn't care. It felt good to be back.

Her checking account had a healthy $3900 balance, and she did not intend to ever be in debt again. She took $200 out of the ATM swearing she would make no additional withdrawals tonight. She played quarter video poker for an hour and had lost $100. She decided she needed a big win if she was going to get to keep playing and quarters wouldn't do it. She decided to try dollar poker. She was down to her last twenty when she was dealt four small cards and the King of Hearts. She held the King and drew to a Royal Flush - $4000, her biggest win ever! She was ecstatic. The only sore spot was the fact that this was a taxable event. She had to provide the casino with her driver's license and social security card. Any win over $1200 was reported to the IRS, which meant she would have to tell Peter about her win. She played a little longer. The dollar machines quickly ate up $200, and she decided to go home – for once a winner.

The next morning at breakfast, her husband was giving her the cold shoulder treatment. However when she pulled out thirty-eight one hundred dollar bills, he forgot their argument and visibly brightened.

He counted the money, "Where'd you get this?" he asked.

"I had a Royal Flush on dollars, I won $4000."

"There's only $3800 here," he said.

"Well, I played a little after I won, in case I was on a hot streak."

"What's this?" he asked, picking up the tax form.

"Anything over $1200 is taxable."

He started peeling off hundred dollar bills, "Okay," he said, "I'll put these away for taxes."

"Not so many, I can claim losses, you know."

"You can't claim $4000 - the IRS would never believe that. Nobody loses that much playing slot machines."

She inwardly groaned, but said, "I know, but I should be able to claim at least $2000. That sounds reasonable."

He gave her back five of the ten bills he had confiscated adding, "If we get audited, you're going to have to pay the taxes, remember."

As soon as Peter left for work, Kim filled out a deposit slip and headed for the bank. She added the $3300 to her existing balance of $3700. She now had $7000 in her checking account. Somehow, she needed to make that make money grow because her husband still believed she had a portfolio of Internet stocks – a portfolio that was growing daily and at a dizzying pace.

Daily she fought the urge to gamble. The seven thousand dollars in her account was enticing her to go to the casino. She was able to stay away for one week. But later in the week, when Peter had an overnight business trip, the allure became too great. "Two hundred dollars," she thought, "and not one penny more."

Nicotine Dreams

On this trip, she didn't even bother with quarters; she headed straight to the dollar machines. Things were quite festive at this bank of machines. Buckets of dollar tokens lined the machines as people hit one four-of-a-kind after another. These were double bonus poker machines. Four identical cards paid, depending on the denomination, between $250 and $800, with maximum coin bet. Kim watched one man who had incredible luck doubling his wins. He would often double several times and as a result he received large hand pays. The machines were jumping and Kim had to wait a few minutes for one to become available. All around her people were winning, lights were flashing, and hoppers were being filled. She could hardly wait to play. She hoped the lucky streaks would last till she got her turn. When she finally sat down, she fed five twenties into her machine. She now had one hundred credits. The machine ate those credits in a few minutes. Kim felt discouraged.

The woman next to her said excitedly, "I've had seven four-of-a-kinds on this machine. I've never been so lucky!"

The woman on the other side of Kim suddenly squealed as she drew four aces for an $800 win.

Kim fed the bill collector her remaining five twenties, trying not to feel angry with the winners surrounding her. She found it difficult to be happy for other people when she was losing herself. Then the magic of last week occurred again. She held one face card and drew a Royal Flush. She was immediately surrounded by people who were attracted by the music her machine was playing. One woman asked her to pat her machine for luck, as if Kim were now some lucky person with the golden touch. She could now add these winnings to her checking account and, even after Peter's IRS cut; her balance would be $10,000. No debts, $10,000, and a 401K plan...YES! YES! YES!

Now, if the damn Internet stocks would just crash, she could become an honest woman again.

"Now, let me get this straight," the ever-analytical Peter said, while counting hundred dollar bills, "twice in two weeks, you held one face card, and you drew to a Royal Flush. The odds of that happening are astronomical. Faulty computer chip, that has to be the answer. There must be something about the way you play coupled with a faulty chip that's allowing you to win all this money."

"It's not a faulty chip," Kim answered, "it's luck. I was due to win, that's all. If they had some faulty chip allowing people to get Royals, the casino would figure that out and fix it."

"I don't know. I'm tempted to give you $500. You could play the same machines; see if you get another Royal. If you win, I get the money, though."

"I can't believe you want to give me money for gambling."

"I know," he said, "I don't really approve of your gambling, however, you are just so damn lucky. How much do you think you've won since you started going out there? Between gambling and your technology stocks, you're getting to be a wealthy woman."

"I don't want to gamble with your money. I just want to quit. I don't want to go to that casino ever again." She gritted her teeth and added, "You know what they say, quit while you're ahead."

Her imaginary portfolio of Internet stocks now exceeded $200,000. She couldn't believe how inflated the stock prices were – they had to crash soon. They had to. In the last two years, since she started going to the casino, she had pretty much lost every cent she had earned. Plus, she had sold about $60.000 in investments to cover her gambling debts. That was bad, but not as bad as lying to her husband and letting him think she had over two hundred grand invested when in fact she had nothing. The stock market tormented her. In the morning she would turn on CNBC. It seemed the NASDAQ could not go down. Every day she prayed for a crash.

She should tell her husband the truth. That revolutionary thought would occasionally pop into her head. After all, what could he do? Divorce her? That would probably be a blessing. She found her marriage oppressive; her husband was controlling and compulsive. She longed for freedom. If they divorced, he would have to give her half of their property. He was worth plenty and she earned good money. She would be fine. No judge would look at her gambling losses; it didn't work that way anymore. This was a no-fault divorce state, just split the assets and don't look at behavior. Especially since no minor children were involved. She knew she would have emotional support if they divorced. She had friends, she had her children, and she had her job. If she could just quit gambling, she would be fine. Maybe without the stress of an unhappy marriage, she wouldn't even want to gamble. It was her husband who would suffer. He had no friends, and his relationship with the kids had always been distant. She thought the kids would understand the divorce. But the gambling - the children did not know about that. What would they think of her if Peter told them? She felt a strong sense of responsibility to her family, and she wanted all of them, even Peter, to admire her. She was embarrassed to show him her weakness, her foolishness. She could stand him hating her, but she could not tolerate him losing respect for her.

And what if he didn't want a divorce? Could she stay with him once he knew what she had done?

Would he ever trust her again? Would he throw this in her face every time they had a disagreement? Her marriage was not strong enough to survive this amount of discord. She kept her mouth shut as she watched the Internet stocks continue to soar.

# Chapter Eleven

Today was her forty-seventh birthday: the two-year anniversary of her first trip to the casino. Like they did every birthday and anniversary, she and Peter went out to dinner. Since it was her birthday, Kim got to choose the restaurant. All day she had been preparing her palate for Mexican food. She knew exactly what she would order: a barbecued burrito, chips, salsa and a strawberry margarita. When they arrived at the restaurant, it was busy and they were told there would be a half-hour wait.

"I'm not waiting half an hour. Let's go somewhere else," Peter said.

Kim suggested they stay and have chips and margaritas in the bar while waiting for a table.

"Have you seen the price of their drinks?" Peter snapped, "We're not having any alcohol tonight. If you want a drink, you can fix one when we get home."

Kim suggested a Tex-Mex restaurant which was twenty minutes away. She could still have chips, salsa and a Diet Coke, no sense getting into an argument. And a fajita that would be almost as good as the burrito. There was a forty-five minute wait at the second restaurant.

As they drove away from that restaurant, Kim suggested a couple of other places she liked.

"What's the point," Peter fumed, "they'll all keep us waiting."

Kim didn't not point out that they could now be eating at the first restaurant if they hadn't wasted so much time driving all over town.

"You know what I'm hungry for?" Peter asked. "White Castles. Haven't had them for years. What do you say? It'll be like we're teenagers again."

While they were eating their hamburgers, Peter brought out a gift-wrapped box. He prided himself on his careless wrapping style. "The man has PhD," Kim thought, "and his packages appear wrapped by a pre-schooler." The paper was bright red and purple decorated with Barney dinosaurs and Christmas trees. He had purchased the paper for only ten cents a roll last January. She complimented him on his wrapping. She had been hinting for a new Coach wallet but the box was rather big and heavy for a billfold. Of course, it would be just like Peter to try to disguise the contents. She unwrapped it quickly; eager to see what he'd gotten her.

Inside was a Dust Buster hand held vacuum cleaner.

"I know you wanted a wallet," Peter said, "and I did plan to get you one. But have you checked out the prices? They're over a hundred dollars. And you really don't need one. There's nothing wrong with the one you have. This is much more practical. You know, I've been noticing the stairs are pretty grungy. This'll do a better job than our big vacuum. Also, there's always sand around the kitty litter box. You could just take this out every day and clean up the litter."

"The kitty litter is you job. It's the only thing you do around the house," Kim complained.

"Yes," Peter answered, "I change the litter, but the floor is your responsibility."

They finished their burger, Kim took a Pepcid and they went home – one more celebration behind them.

Two weeks later it was Peter's birthday and Kim's turn to treat.

"Do you want to have White Castles again?" Kim asked.

"No," Peter answered, "I can wait a few years before eating them again. Your birthday was a disaster with all that waiting. For my birthday I'd like to be smart. I'm going to make reservations at a decent restaurant so our table will be ready when we arrive."

Their table wasn't ready, but since Kim was designated driver and paying the tab, Peter thought they should have a drink in the bar while they waited. He had a martini, she a Diet Coke. For dinner he ordered shrimp cocktail, filet mignon, and a "good" wine the steward recommended. For dessert he had a crème brulee followed by brandy. While Peter was sipping his drink, Kim presented him with his gift, a subscription to the "Tightwad Gazette". He was very pleased. The bill came to $102. Peter complained that Kim left too large a tip.

"Fifteen percent is perfectly adequate," he said, "I don't know why you left twenty dollars."

Kim didn't know why they couldn't have had a birthday like hers. If he was sick of White Castle, there was always McDonalds's.

# Chapter Twelve

Kim was really trying to keep away from the casino, but staying away completely seemed impossible. Part of the problem was that her friends all liked to gamble. It seemed every time they made plans to do one thing, they ended up gambling instead. The other activities that used to give them pleasure now seemed boring. Lunch, movies, shopping, the standard housewife diversions, these now seemed mundane next to the adrenaline rush they would receive at the casino. Pat especially liked going there for she, like Kim, was a closet smoker.

They would head out to the casino in the morning, planning the story they would tell their husbands at the end of the day. They didn't want to really lie so they figured out stories that would contain a grain of truth. As they passed through the suburb of Wayzata, Pat would say, "We could tell them we went to Wayzata today." When they stopped to buy cigarettes, they would decide to tell them they had gone shopping. On the rare occasions when they left the casino with any money they would often stop and buy a Dairy Queen on the way home.

On those days, they could honestly say they had gone out to lunch. Sometimes they did resort to blatant lies, like saying they had been to a movie. They would check the paper for the correct time and theater, then read a review on the Internet so they would have a story line to share with their husbands. Their stories often would become quite complex, and they would trust each other to keep the lies straight and to cover for each other.

They were invariably upbeat and optimistic on the drive to the casino, looking for signs that today they'd be lucky. Their first stop was always at a Seven-Eleven where they would get their cigarettes. They then drove the thirty-one miles with car windows rolled down despite the weather, puffing on cigarettes, trying to keep the smoke smell out of the car. They started buying little green pine scented trees to hang from their rearview mirrors.

Coming home was different story. It was extremely rare for either of them to have been a winner, and it was almost unheard of that they both would be ahead. The usual scenario was that they both had lost and that one owed the other forty or fifty dollars. The conversation on the drive home never varied.

"That was stupid."

"Let's never go there again."

"It's not even any fun."

Their resolve to quit gambling would last only until they had a little freedom and some available money.

The trips to the casino with Pat took a steady toll on Kim's finances, but the real damage was always done when she went to the casino alone. These trips usually occurred when Peter was out of town. She would go to the casino late after receiving Peter's check-in phone call. She often didn't return home until Peter was expected to call again, or until he was due home. It was always a strain to act as if she had stayed home during his absence and to pretend she was well rested and that nothing notable had taken place. In fact, she had often lost thousands of dollars while he was on business trips.

Behind her smiling face, she would panic. She was overwhelmed by her losses and her lack of control. She could not stop gambling. She continued to go to the casino always praying for a win. She wrote checks, hit the ATM, and got cash advances on her credit cards. In no time her $10,000 checking account balance was depleted and she was back in debt. Now, there was no more stock to sell. Her assets were zero. Her only resource was her 401K which she didn't dare touch. And to make matters worse, the stock market continued to set new records almost daily.

She now owed over $25,000 dollars on her ready reserve and credit cards. She was feeling lower than she had ever felt before. She worried about money constantly, even started picking up extra shifts at work. There seemed no way out. As she sat at the dinner table ruminating about her money concerns, her husband, who had been puffed up like a chicken all evening, told her his good news.

"I've been selected to participate in an international program. I'll be going to Europe for at least one week out of every month."

Kim felt sick. Much as her husband annoyed her, his presence did have a stabilizing effect. She had to be home when he was home. She had to have dinner on the table at seven. She had to pick up after him and do his laundry. He was a lot of work and occupied a great deal of her time, but with him gone for a whole week she knew she would lose all the external controls that limited her gambling. She couldn't fathom the amount of trouble she could get into during a week of total freedom. And this was to occur every month. She tried to subdue her rising panic and concentrate on what her husband was saying. She realized she had tuned out everything he was saying.

"And the greatest part," Peter continued, "is that every month a different country will host the meetings. One month I'll be in France, the next Germany, then maybe England. It will be great. I'll get to see the world and eat authentic international cuisine, all on the company's dollar."

Kim thought she would vomit and her eyes filled with tears. She needed this man like she had never needed anyone before.

"Please," she pleaded, "let me go with you."

"I don't know, it's a business trip after all. A wife may seem awkward. I imagine we'll be going out as a group for dinner at night and, of course, I'll be at meetings all day. Are you crying?" he asked.

"A week – you've never been gone that long."
Peter looked puzzled, "I always thought you enjoyed my traveling. I thought you viewed these trips as a vacation from me. I thought you'd be pleased."

"Little trips, yes, but not a week. I don't want you gone that long. What will I do without you here?" Kim sobbed.

Peter's lips formed a sweet smile and his eyes took on a tenderness Kim had rarely seen. He took his wife into his arms and stroked her hair.

"I'll miss you too," he said, "I'll miss you terribly."

And with a sadness that was unbearable, she looked in her husband's eyes and saw that he actually loved her. He had misinterpreted her tears. She didn't want to be with him, she just needed him be her babysitter and policeman. She wondered what their marriage might have been like if she had shown him more warmth. If only she could have viewed his eccentricities with a sense of humor and had been able to stand up to him instead of always kowtowing and then feeling angry. Her marriage was miserable, but perhaps it wasn't all Peter's fault. Her betrayal of him now seemed even worse.

"I'll tell you what," Peter said, "I'll go to this meeting alone. If it seems feasible to take you, I'll let you come on the next trip."

The following week was busy. There was much to do to prepare for Peter's trip – suits to be brought to the cleaner, shoes to be shined and new ties and a garment bag to be purchased. Finally, the day arrived for him to fly to Paris. He called her from the frequent flier club at the airport. He was all business, saying he had some last minute instructions for her. He then told her he had posted three checklists in the house and she was to check them every time she went out. He didn't want her to forget to turn down the heat, to lock the doors, to check the stove and the iron to make sure weren't left on, etc. All the tenderness of the preceding week was forgotten. Ten minutes after they hung up, Kim was en route to the casino.

# Chapter Thirteen

It was January, and everything they say about Minnesota winters is true. Kim was freezing despite her hot flashes. It didn't help that her windows were rolled down because she was smoking. As she sped down the freeway at sixty-five miles an hour with the wind whipping through her car, she was sure she felt icicles forming in her nostrils. Plan, plan, plan... Kim was sure there was a way to beat the machines. She needed a system and she needed to stick to it. Her problem, she decided, was that she played too many machines that had poor payoffs. She would stick to machines that she knew, machines she had won on before. When these machines got cold she would go play lower stakes and return to the good machines later, after they'd had time to warm up. She knew exactly what machine she would begin with, and nothing was going to make her throw her money away on something else.

Within minutes of entering the casino she spotted her machine, the one she was determined to play and was dismayed to see a woman bent over it. She went closer, trying to see the number of credits the woman had left - the woman had no credits – she was asleep.

She was asleep at Kim's machine, her head resting on the table-like surface, her arm out-stretched, fingers brushing the coin slot. Now what? Kim would not hesitate to ask someone to move who was just sitting at her machine; after all, there were seats everywhere. But sleeping..... Also, the woman was black. She may think Kim a racist if she were to arouse her. She asked people playing nearby if they were with her. No such luck.

"How long has she been sleeping?" she asked.

"Over an hour," came the reply.

She waited fifteen minutes. Finally, unable to sit without playing any longer, she tapped the sleeping woman on the shoulder.

"Can I get you a room, dear? You're sound asleep at my machine. I have plenty of comps, and if you would just get up I'd gladly get you one."

The drowsy woman declined the room and stumbled off. Kim took possession of the machine. She hung her coat on the back of the chair and got two Diet Cokes and an extra book of matches at the concession stand. She checked her cigarettes. She had a full pack, plus three. She emptied an overflowing ashtray and put it next to her machine. Kim placed a cup on the seat of her chair and placed her player card in its slot. She slid a twenty into the slot machine's bill collector, then asked the person next to her to watch her machine while she went to the bathroom. Once all her needs were met, she was ready to play. "It's all in your mood," she told herself. "Be upbeat and confident - make yourself comfortable and don't rush."

She was fairly lucky on this machine. She didn't win, but lost slowly. She sat between two women who were talkative and in good spirits. They all chatted and Kim found herself having a good time. One of the women mentioned that she had four toy poodles.

"I've always wanted a dog," Kim said, "but my husband doesn't think he likes dogs. We have two cats. They were strays. I don't really like them, but my husband is crazy about them. I know he'd like a dog if we had one. It's just he's never been around dogs."

"Why don't you just bring a puppy home," the other lady asked. "What could he do about it? You have every right to do what you want."

Kim noticed this woman was not wearing a wedding ring.

The thought of buying a puppy was appealing. She could tell Peter that the dog was a stray, and that she kept it because she was so lonely. She could tell him the dog would be great protection since Peter was so frequently out of town. A dog would keep her at home. A puppy would be like having a baby in the house. She had been so happy when her children were little, but now they were all grown up and didn't seem to need her at all. "Tomorrow," she thought, "maybe tomorrow she would get herself a dog."

Tomorrow came, but no puppy was purchased for Kim was still at the casino. She was no longer thinking about puppies or Peter or anything else except money. At home she worried about money incessantly and about all the money she had lost. She worried about it at the casino too, but there she worried that she wouldn't be able to get her hands on more money so she could keep playing. She was depressed and anxious. Kim no longer visited with other gamblers. Her mood was sour, and she was resentful when other people won. Occasionally, she would win $250 or $400, and people would congratulate her over these wins, calling her "lucky." She would wave them off, showing little enjoyment, complaining that these wins were not enough. She needed ten more of them. She needed a Royal Flush. She had lost so much that these little jackpots meant nothing. She had been gambling for twenty-six hours. Her head ached and her stomach hurt. She hadn't eaten. She had smoked four packs of cigarettes and had developed a deep cough. Peter was supposed to call today. She wasn't sure what time he'd call as he was on European time. She had lost $4000. It was time to go home.

The phone was ringing as she entered the dark house – it was Peter.

"Hi," he said, "I'm having a great time. It was really hard staying awake today for my meeting, between jet lag and wine with lunch. Man, all I wanted to do was sleep. But Paris is beautiful. I plan to do a little sight seeing tonight. We're having a dinner cruise tonight on the Seine - Paris is all lit up at night - it should be spectacular. How are things at home? What are you doing? Are the cats okay?"

"The cats are fine," Kim answered. "And me, I'm fine, just doing the usual stuff, I guess."

"I'm glad everything is okay. I need you to do some things for me. I want you to check all the ads for dry cleaning coupons and find the cheapest place, then bring my wool blanket in to be cleaned so it'll be back when I get home. I need handkerchiefs ironed for work next week. I had to pack everyone that was in my drawer. I also want you to bring my heavy work boots to the shoe shop for new soles."

"Those boots are twenty years old," Kim complained, "why don't you just throw them out?'

"That's the difference between you and me, Kim. I make things last. You're just a spendthrift. And while you're out running errands, stop at Cub and get a ham - they're on sale. Try to make all the stops in one outing so you can save on gas. Get organized, know where you plan to go, have your coupons ready, remember… save money, save money."

Kim coughed loudly.

"You sound like you're catching a cold," Peter said, "I hope not. I can't afford to catch any colds from you. With all this traveling my immune system will be weakened. Be healthy by the time I get home."

They said "goodnight" and Kim went to bed.

Kim tossed and turned until four in the morning. She wondered when she last bathed, it seemed days ago. She could smell stale smoke on herself. She got up, took a bath and got dressed. She hadn't planned to do that, it was as if her body was in autopilot, and she had no control over it. It was a new day for her credit cards. They were her only remaining source of money. Her checking account balance was overdrawn to its ready reserve maximum. She still had several thousand available on her credit cards, which she could use for cash advances. She returned to the casino. She didn't return home for three days.

She took out the maximum she could withdraw on her two cards. Kim knew she had more money available, but cash advances were limited at the casino. If she lost all this, she could go to a bank in the morning and take out additional funds. She no longer planned to win. That happy feeling of expectation she used to have when driving to the casino was gone. She had become quite pessimistic about her gambling. She now knew she would lose – she just didn't know how much.

She got her money then headed for the smoke shop.

"Five packs of Carlton 120's and ten books of matches, please."

"We have a special on lighters, would you like one?"

"No thanks," Kim answered, "I don't smoke."

"Could have fooled me," the clerk said.

"Well, I smoke when I'm here, but I don't normally smoke. I'm not really committed to smoking. A lighter seems like a commitment."

"I don't know," the clerk said, "seems like you're here enough to have gone through several lighters."

She glared at him. He counted out the matches and Kim left, in search of a lucky machine.

Her cash advance was gone before the banks opened, and for the first time Kim wrote a check she knew would bounce. She'd figure a way to cover it before that happened, she thought.

She decided to play some nickel slot machines. The dollar poker held better chances for a big win, but the wins were few and far between. Better to make her money last longer by playing low stakes. The new slot machines were fun. You usually played nine lines and there was often a second screen where you could try to win additional money. She started slow, playing one coin per line. Her credits were going fast, but she felt due to win so she upped her bet-per-line. She was soon playing max bet, which was ten coins per line. She fed twenty after twenty into the bill collector. It occurred to her she was now betting $4.50 per spin - so much for low stakes. She might as well play dollars. She returned to her favorite machines, the double bonus poker. Her money was gone by morning, so she drove to the bank and put another $5000 on her credit cards. She returned to the casino and to her dollar poker machines.

She moved from machine to machine, having no luck. She played all day and well into the night. She hadn't eaten for a day. The combination of cigarettes and lack of food had given her a splitting headache. She had lost $2000 of the $5000. Every time she left a machine, someone else would sit down and win big. She was getting angry. She decided she would quit moving around and instead stay at one machine and wait for it to start paying.

She picked a machine she felt was due to hit. She sunk her remaining $3000 into this machine. She got nothing back. How is that even possible? It had to be due; nothing could stay this cold for this long! It was the middle of the night and she'd been playing this machine for hours. She knew it would hit if she could just play a little longer, but she had no way to get her hands on any more money. She had now exceeded her ready reserve limit by $2000. She had never done this before and she didn't know how she'd be able to cover the overdraft. She was hoping her bank would give her a personal loan although she was afraid when they looked at all the checks written to the casino and all the ATM withdrawals, they would view her as a poor credit risk.

She thought she'd try the ATM again, even though she realized it was hopeless. The expected message flashed on the screen, "Daily limit has been reached." She stared at the message unable to walk away from the ATM. As she stood there immobilized, she heard music in the distance, the music the machines play when someone has won a jackpot. She looked in the direction of the sound and saw lights flashing on the machine she had just left. She couldn't stop herself; she walked back to the machine and saw an overjoyed woman sitting in front of a Royal Flush - she had just won $4000 on Kim's machine.

Kim felt weak and nauseated. She hurried to the bathroom as she felt stomach acid rise in her throat. She barely got into a stall before she started throwing up all the Diet Coke she had consumed. Once her stomach was empty, Kim unzipped her pants and sat down on the toilet. She sat there with her pants down and her head in her hands, wondering how she had sunk so low. "I must hate myself," she thought. "There's no other explanation."

# Chapter Fourteen

She had no choice but to go home. She had been at the casino for forty-eight hours. She had lost $9000 and was physically ill. It was four in the morning and bitterly cold. The temperature was well below zero with the wind chill, and she knew she'd have a miserable walk to her car. "Wind chill," she thought, "don't we suffer enough with life the way it is, do we have to add in additional misery quotients such as wind chills?" She buttoned up her long black coat, pulled a stocking cap over her head, and donned her heavy winter gloves. Despite the cold she walked slowly to her car, her energy level at an all time low. A woman walking rapidly soon surpassed her - it was the woman who had won the jackpot, the woman who had won Kim's money. This woman must be the luckiest woman alive, not only was she a winner, she was parked close to the door.

Kim called to her, "Would you mind giving me a lift to my car? I'm parked way at the back of the lot and I'm freezing. I'm afraid I'm getting sick."

The woman looked at Kim and took pity on her. She did look sick. She certainly wasn't afraid of Kim;

Katie Cunningham

middle-aged women do not fear each other, not physically anyway.

"Of course, hop in. Hope you don't mind sitting here for a minute, I don't like to drive until my car warms up a little."

"That's fine, it beats being out in that wind. By the way, congratulations on your big win. I saw you hit a Royal on dollars," Kim said. "Aren't you nervous walking out in this deserted parking lot with that much cash on you?"

"What's to be afraid of? There's no one out here but you - plus, I have this," she said, showing Kim the tiny revolver she was holding in her hand.

"Please," Kim said. "Put that down, you're making me nervous."

"Sorry," the woman said, placing the gun on the console between them.

"You know," Kim told the woman, "I'd been playing that machine all night. Lost a bundle in it. Never gave me anything."

"Well, that's gambling for you," the woman answered, "You just never know when a machine will hit."

"Maybe, but I knew that machine was going to hit. It was so overdue," Kim said. "How much had you put in when you drew the Royal?"

"That's the great part," she answered, "I only slid in a five dollar bill 'cause I was only going to play one hand. The crazy thing is, it dealt me that Royal, I didn't even have to draw for it." The woman laughed.

Suddenly Kim was filled with rage. This woman had stolen $4000 from her and was laughing about it.

"That was my money you won, I don't see what's so funny!"

"That wasn't your money, what are you talking about," the woman answered, sounding annoyed.

"It was my money. Three thousand dollars, I put $3000 in that machine. You owe me something! Lend me some money, a loan, that's all I want from you... just a loan."

"I think you better get out of my car right now!" the woman said, fear creeping into her voice.

"You've stolen my money and now you won't even give me a ride to my car. What kind of person are you? If you had an ounce of decency you would lend me some of that money so I could go in there and win back what I've lost."

"Listen, I think you're one sick cookie and I want you out of my car right now. I haven't stolen anything from you. I owe you nothing and I think you should get some help for your gambling problem."

"Please," Kim cried, "$100, that's all I ask. My luck is bound to change. Just give me a chance."

"I'm not giving you any money. I think you're nuts. I won that money fair and square!"

"Please, please," Kim pleaded, "can't you see how desperate I am? One hundred dollars, that's all, that's all I ask. If I hadn't put all that money in that machine, it would never have hit like that. You owe me!"

The woman, now looking really afraid, picked up the gun, pointed it at Kim and yelled, "Get out of my car right now!"

"Don't point that thing at me," Kim screamed, and without thinking, she grabbed it out of the woman's hand.

The shocked woman offered no resistance.

Kim waved the gun in the woman's face. She was shaking, she was crying, she was begging, "Please, just $100, please, just give me a chance."

The gun bounced up and down in Kim's hand, as she gestured wildly, punctuating her words with her hands. She looked like a psychotic person conducting an orchestra and the little gun was her baton.

"Please, please…" she cried. Every shred of self-respect had left her. She felt she was fighting for her life.

The gun went off. Kim didn't think she had pulled the trigger; it just seemed to fire independently. She stared at the woman, waiting for her head to explode. Nothing much happened, except a small hole, like a third eye, formed in the middle of the woman's forehead. Kim thought she heard the sound of a bullet ricocheting within the confines of the woman's skull. "This can't be happening," Kim thought. "I must be hallucinating from lack of sleep." Scenes from David Lynch and Quentin Tarantino films flashed through her head. She feared she was cracking up.

She looked at the woman, "Are you okay?" she whispered.

The woman didn't answer - just stared at Kim with three sightless eyes.

Kim felt herself regressing into the comfortable age where peek-a-boo was magic. "If I can't see you - you don't exist." She pushed the woman down as far as could on the seat and covered her with a blanket she found on the backseat. The woman disappeared. Kim returned the gun to the woman's purse, took the cash, locked the car and returned to the casino.

# Chapter Fifteen

She couldn't lose.

Kim had decided to try something new. They had recently installed Triple Bonus Poker, where you had to have a pair of kings or better to win. The payoffs for four-of-a-kind were incredible. She slipped a twenty into the machine and was immediately dealt four deuces. She had just won $600. She continued to play this machine and continued to hit. She had never had such luck. Her buckets of dollar tokens were taking up every available inch of space on the bank of machines.

When the line at the cashier's cage was short, she would carry over a few buckets and exchange them for hundred dollar bills. Each bucket held $400 and right now there were ten of them lined up. When her machine eventually died, she moved to the adjoining machine where her luck continued. She glanced at her watch. It was three in the morning, and she had been playing and winning for the twenty-three hours that had elapsed since she had returned to the casino.

She was due at work in four hours, and Peter was due home tonight. She cashed in all her buckets and asked someone to hold her machine for her while she went in search of a payphone. She finally found one that was removed from the casino noise. She had to call in sick to work, and she didn't want the sound of slot machines to be heard in the background. She told the charge nurse she wouldn't be in, that she had a cold. Her raspy smoker's voice and cough made the story sound feasible.

She returned to her machine and to winning. She had a great time; laughing, smoking, and chatting with other players. "This is what gambling is all about," she thought. "This thrill of winning, the adrenaline rush when you have a big hit." She couldn't remember ever having had so much fun.

She checked the time; Peter would be home in seven hours. She hadn't run any of the errands he had assigned her and the house was a mess. She cashed in her tokens and flew out the door. She bought the ham on her way home. She ran into the house, threw a load of laundry in the washer, then grabbed Peter's boots and blanket and rushed back to her car. She hadn't bothered looking for dry cleaning ads; instead she just went to the expensive dry cleaner that would do your cleaning immediately. She told them she needed the blanket back this afternoon.

Next she brought the boots to the shoemaker and told him she'd pay triple if he'd do the job today. She returned home, put the clothes in the dryer, turned on the iron and faced the handkerchiefs. She rushed around the house doing a desultory job of cleaning, for once grateful to have a dust buster. She folded the clothes as she took them out of the dryer, then raced out the door and sped to the drycleaners and shoe repair shop. Once all the errands were completed she summoned up her courage and looked in the mirror. She was wreck, with dirty hair and smudged three-day-old make-up. Her face and hands were filthy from handling all the coins and from touching her face. She hadn't brushed her teeth for three days. She took a quick shower, washed her hair, put on some make-up, and was just curling her hair when she heard the door open. Peter was home.

"What the hell is going on around here?" he shouted. "I've been calling for three days, where have you been?"

Thinking quickly, Kim answered, "The phone, the phone's been out of order. They just fixed it today."

"Why didn't you leave a message for me at work? You know you can do that. I've been frantic with worry – and why aren't you at work?'

"I've been sick," Kim said, "I have a cold. I felt so crummy - I just forgot to call you."

"Well… you do look sick," Peter said, really looking at her for the first time. "Keep away from me - I don't want to catch it."

They visited for a while at a distance, Peter wanting to talk about his trip. Kim was blurry-eyed but attempted to listen to him. Finally Peter said he going to bed and as she heard his bedroom door shut, she thought she would finally be able to stop the charade and relax. She felt physically ill. Her head throbbed and her stomach ached. She was so tired that she was hallucinating and she kept imagining bugs and rodents running along the walls. There are no bugs, she told herself, it's just sleep deprivation. There's nothing to be scared of.

She rummaged through her medicine cabinet and found Excedrin and she took two for her headache. She also took two Motrin in case the Excedrin didn't work. She took a Pepcid for the hole she felt forming in her stomach lining, and a Benadryl to help her sleep. "All symptoms covered," she thought, "except for the sound of slot machines." She couldn't get those out of her head. The cacophony in her ears was as loud as if she were sitting in the casino. She slipped on her night-gown and went to bed. Her body was exhausted. How long had it been since she'd slept? Her mind, however, was wide-awake. The slot machines were deafening. She craved a cigarette. "Concentrate on the money," she thought. Concentrate on all she had won. The need for nicotine finally overwhelmed her and she left her bed to get a cigarette or Nicorette gum. Neither was to be found, but she did locate a box of Nicotine patches. Kim peeled the backing off one and slapped it on her upper thigh. "Now," she prayed, "just let me sleep."

She awoke to a crushing pain in her chest. She felt her blood pressure rising and silently cursed her doctor who had told her you couldn't feel an increase in blood pressure. She thought she was having a heart attack or a stroke. Breathing became difficult, and she could feel her heart beat and hear the blood rush through her head. It was the dreams that had awakened her; horri-ble dreams filled with violence, blood, and an extreme paranoia that someone was after her. "It's the patch," she thought, "it gives me nightmares. I shouldn't use it at night." She tried to calm herself and reassure herself that there was no reason for her to dream of death and injury, of bodies in cars.... bodies in cars...bodies in cars.... "Oh my God," she thought, "what have I done?"

During the next week her life took on all the as-pects of a nightmare. She thought she was losing her mind. She felt she had fallen into the same abyss that had taken her patients' sanity. She had suffered from insomnia since the beginning of menopause; now the little sleep she was able to attain was riddled with dreams of cars in parking lots, of dead women in those cars. Awake she would try to rid herself of these thoughts, constantly seeking to distract herself. She called friends frequently and would talk nonstop, in a manic fashion, in the subconscious hope that idle prattle would block the visions passing through her brain. Kim never actually believed these visions and morbid thoughts were based in reality; she had repressed and denied to herself the events that had taken place in the Jackpot Casino parking lot. To her, that night existed only as a bad dream. Her psyche would not allow her to face the truth. Only in her sleep did she relive that awful moment in the convoluted, confusing style of dreams.

Sometimes she would awaken, hearing herself cry, "It was an accident, that's all, a terrible accident."

And some voice, would say, as she drifted in that place between sleep and awakening, "You shot her in the forehead with her own fucking gun and you stole her money. Tell me Kim – how was that an accident?"

# Chapter Sixteen

Another birthday loomed on the horizon. She would be forty-eight this weekend. Birthdays now did not mark her years on earth but rather her years of gambling. Only three years. That was all it had taken to destroy her, to turn her into a lying, tormented person she could no longer recognize. The only place she was still able to function as a productive and caring person was at work.

And at work was where she spent that birthday. Her coworkers, always seeking a way to make the job more festive, had provided chips, salsa, candy and a birthday cake in her honor. All the staff had signed a funny card for Kim. She had difficulty showing an appropriate reaction as she read it. The patients, that day, were not in a festive mood. They were agitated and surly. Finally, a patient totally lost it. He began throwing chairs in the lounge and was threatening anyone who got near him. Below a sign which read "beam me up Scotty" was a panic button which Kim hit as she rushed from the nursing station to the dayroom. This alerted security that psych needed immediate help. After the patient was subdued, medicated, and placed in seclusion, the security guards went in the back room to have some birthday cake. It was fortunate that they had remained on the unit because a fight suddenly broke out between two of the patients. The ICU felt like the cathouse at the zoo: too many tigers and too little room.

As the unit finally settled, the admissions started. It was to be a very busy day. Kim admitted a young man who had been sent over from the jail where he had made a suicide attempt. He was in jail for murdering his parents, though he was on drugs at the time and claimed to be unaware of his actions. As his mind cleared from the drugs and he learned what he had done, he had become despondent and suicidal. Kim's heart broke for this young man. When she commented to her coworker, Steve, how sorry she felt for this patient, Steve exploded.

"For God's sake, Kim, this kid just wasted his family! How can you possibly feel sorry for him? He's a slime ball."

"But he didn't mean to." Kim said, "He wasn't in his right mind at the time. You can't blame him; you have to look at intent. He didn't intend to kill his family."

"Intent! His parents are dead. Doesn't make much difference to them what his 'intent' was, that won't bring them back. Plus, what do you think his intent was as he shot his mother in the chest and his father in the head? I would say his intent was pretty clear."

That cloud of oppressive guilt that had been following Kim since her husband's trip to France once again enveloped her. She wondered if she would now begin to feel guilt just because she felt compassion for a young murderer. The image of a parked car flashed in her brain. She shook her head to clear her thoughts and bit her lip as she tried to keep herself from crying.

"Don't get mad at me Steve," she begged. "It's my birthday, be nice."

"Sorry," Steve said. "I just get so mad at all these scumbags." He smiled. "I brought you some chocolate."

As Kim sat at the nursing station, writing up her admission and eating the Hershey Kisses Steve had given her, she thought of what he had told her on his last birthday.

"My birthday gift to myself is to be guilt-free for fifteen minutes a day," he had said.

Kim was puzzled. "What do you have to feel guilty about?"

"I'm Jewish," he answered.

She never did understand that explanation, but she did understand the feeling – the feeling of ever-present guilt that made any form of joy impossible. Steve was a good guy, he should be happy with himself, but she... she was a gambler and a liar. She had lost vast sums of money, and something else... something else was torturing her, something she didn't want to think about.

The following day at work was quite pleasant. Because of all the turmoil on Saturday, a lot of medication had been given resulting in a much quieter unit on Sunday. Two young black men from the jail asked Kim and another nurse, Mindy, to play Spades with them.

"You understand," Eugene, the older of the two patients, said, "this is a penitentiary game. We don't 'spect you white suburban gals are going to do too good, so we'll do a practice hand. Ya know, kinda show you the rules."

Kim and Mindy, who had played plenty of Spades during their years working psych, joined the two men. The men hurried and sat across from each other, not wanting to be stuck with the women as partners. The women were dealt good cards and they played skill-fully. They took every trick.

Mindy smiled and said, "If you don't mind my saying..."

"I do mind," Kabal answered.

"You don't even know what I was going to say."

"You were going to say you whipped our black asses," Eugene answered.

"I don't think I would have chosen those words," Mindy said.

"The sentiment's right, though," Kim laughed.
Kabal got up from the table, "we need a CON-sul-ta-tion," he said to Eugene, motioning for him to join him a few feet away.

They put their heads together for a couple of min-utes and then returned to the table.

"It doesn't seem right, us playing this way, you know, men against women, black against white, it ain't...mmm... what's the word I want?"

"Politically correct?" Kim asked.

"Right, it ain't PC," Eugene smiled.

They teamed up again. Now it was Kim and Kabal against Mindy and Eugene. They were evenly matched and the games were interesting.

While they were playing, the women started chat-ting about Mindy's new house, a conversation that seemed to exclude the two men.

Eugene silenced them by saying, "This is Spades, and we don't talk while playing. The only sounds al-lowed while playing Spades are the sounds of mice running across the floor and cockroaches skittering up the walls. Understand?"

These images put a damper on the women's con-versation for a while. The next to start speaking was Kabal.

"I wish I lived in your neighborhoods," he said.

"Maybe you will some day, when you're older, have a job," Kim said.

Kabal looked at her as if she were from Mars.

"I don't think so."

"Have you ever thought of getting some training?" Kim asked, "So that someday you could have a better life? You're only nineteen and you're a smart, good looking guy. Have you thought about what you'd really like to do for a living?"

Kabal looked embarrassed, but answered the question. "If I could be anything in the world, I'd be a plumber."

Mindy and Kim looked at each other, surprised. They tried to keep from smiling. Not a rap star or a professional athlete - Kabal wanted to be a plumber.

"That seems to be a reasonable goal," Mindy said, "Maybe you should look into going to a Vo-Tech school. I'm sure there's some sort of classes you could take."

"Look," he answered, "I ain't never going to be no plumber. Look at my family – they're a bunch of homicidal nutcases. Half of them are in jail and the other half committed."

Kim knew this was true as several of his family members had been her patients. She knew there was… How do they say it… No lifeguard in his gene pool.

"And another thing," he went on. "I've been in a gang since I was nine. You know, you only leave my gang one way. I've already been shot twice, and the second time was by my own mother. I ain't never going to live in no suburb and I ain't never going to be no plumber."

Kabal didn't have much, but he did have insight

# Chapter Seventeen

When Kim finally got home from her twelve-hour shift she was exhausted but, as usual, was unable to sleep. She tried to read, she tried to watch TV, but she was constantly distracted by her thoughts. Her mind seemed to have a mind of it own...h-m-m-m...and she had no control over the myriad of thoughts bouncing about in her brain. And then there was the anxiety, an ever-abiding anxiety that constricted her chest and caused her head to ache. At five A.M. she took a Benadryl and finally fell asleep.

She was awakened by a loud knocking on the door. She looked out the window and saw a nondescript car parked in her driveway, Jehovah's Witnesses she guessed, and went back to bed. The knocking continued, louder than ever. She gave up trying to sleep, put on a robe, and answered the door. Two large, formidable men stood at the door wearing inexpensive suits with ties that clashed. "These are no Jehovah Witnesses," she thought, her concern growing. They flashed badges at her and introduced themselves as Detectives Anderson and Wright. She invited them in, wishing as she did that the house were tidier and that she was dressed.

"Sorry to disturb you, ma'am. It's nine o'clock, sorta figured you'd be up." Detective Wright said.

Kim felt they were already passing judgment on her and she didn't even know why they were here. They soon told her.

"We understand you spent a lot of time at Jackpot Casino week before last. Couple days ago we found a woman's body in her car in their parking lot. Seems she was killed during the time you were in the casino. The body had been in that car for a long time. Between the casino and hotel, cars can sit in that lot for quite awhile before someone takes notice. The cold weather makes pinpointing the exact time of death difficult but we're pretty sure it happened while you were out there. Maybe you've already heard about it."

"Oh my God," Kim thought, "just like in her dreams."

"No," she answered, looking visibly shaken. "I worked all weekend, didn't get a chance to read the paper or watch much TV."

The policemen noted her discomfiture, Detective Anderson remarked, "You seem pretty nervous about it, can you tell us why?"

"Well, a woman's dead," Kim answered. "That's upsetting. And I'm worried about you being here. I have a gambling problem and I don't want my husband to find out."

"Sounds like you were there for days. They monitor these things you know. You took out money and you used your player's card. How could you have been there all that time without your husband knowing?" Detective Wright asked.

"He was on a business trip in Europe. He was gone almost a week. I had lost a lot of money and I needed to stay till I won it back. I did get it all back, you can check. I got really lucky and then I went home.

I'm really trying to quit," she said, almost in tears. "My husband won't have to find out about this, will he?"

"Where do you get your money for gambling?"

"I work, I'm a nurse. I worked last night, that's why I was still sleeping."

"What we want to know is if you saw anything suspicious while you were playing. If you noticed anyone behaving oddly or taking an unusual interest in the people who were winning."

"I didn't notice anything odd," Kim said, "I don't really pay attention to much when I gamble, just my machine. I guess that's part of my problem – I get too focused on my gambling, it makes me oblivious to everything, but then, maybe that's why I do it."

Detective Wright handed her a business card, "If you think of anything, let us know. We may have to contact you again. We'll try to be discreet. At this point, we don't need to involve you husband in this. And…ah…" he added softly, "you might want to think about getting help for you problem."

They wished her a good day and apologized for waking her.

Kim watched through her living room windows as they backed their car out of the driveway. They almost hit her trash which was sitting on the curb waiting to be collected. Kim suddenly wanted to be rid of all the clothes she had worn during the time that the woman was killed. She wanted no reminders of that terrible occurrence. She took out a large plastic garbage bag and stuffed it full with the pants, sweater, boots, coat, hat and gloves she was wearing two weeks ago. She set the bag on the curb, grateful to have them out of her house and out of her life.

That night at dinner Peter, always the news junkie, brought up the body found in the casino parking lot. "I don't suppose you read yesterday's paper?" he asked.

"A woman was murdered at Jackpot Casino. Her body was left in her car. They didn't even find her body for several days. Guess her family had reported her missing and had given the police her license plate number, that's how she was finally found. Seems she spent a lot of time at the casino, according to the paper, her family claims they didn't even know she gambled. Paper says it was an apparent robbery – she had won a lot that night but no money was found in the car. She had been shot in the head...terrible, terrible. I hope you remember this if you ever plan to go that place again. It's not safe for a woman to be going out alone to places like that."

Kim thought she heard a buzzing sound. She tried to remember the Emily Dickinson poem, something about: *I heard a fly buzz when I died.* She wondered if she was dying, she wondered if she was glad about it – if it were true.

"Kim – Earth to Kim, I'm talking to you – can you hear me? You're sitting there like some kind of zombie, what's the matter with you, anyway?"

"I'm sorry, Peter," Kim answered, "I have a headache. Makes concentrating difficult."

"It seems like you're sick all the time lately. Maybe you should see your doctor."

"Maybe I will," Kim said, "Maybe I could get something to help with menopause."

"I'm certainly in favor of that." Peter said. "I'm tired of living in an icebox, and I'm tired of how weird you've gotten. You're always hot, you're always tired, you never sleep, you're always preoccupied like your mind's somewhere else, you never feel good, you get upset so easily – you really should see your doctor. There is definitely something wrong with you. Tonight you better get a good night's sleep, for a change. After you clean up the kitchen, you should go right to bed."

"Right."

Once the kitchen was tidy, she went upstairs to their home office, she logged onto the Internet to check on her fantasy portfolio - $287,965 – shit. As she was signing off, the phone rang. It was Pat.

"Did you hear about the murder at Jackpot Casino? It had to have happened when Jim was in France. I bet you were there when she got whacked."

"Whacked? Jesus, Pat."

"Do you think you know who she is? Have you seen her out there? The paper said she went there often – go look at the paper, her picture's in it."

"I don't want to talk about this, it's unpleasant," Kim said.

"What do you mean, unpleasant? Since when are you so squeamish? You love this stuff. You work with murderers for God's sake."

"This is different. This is too close to home. That could have been me in the parking lot. I don't want to think about it."

"It couldn't have been you," Pat laughed. "It was a robbery, remember? When did you ever leave that casino with something worth stealing?"

"I've left there plenty of times with money. I won that week. I don't want to talk about this anymore; I'm going to bed. Goodnight."

# Chapter Eighteen

In an attempt to keep busy, Kim called her daughter the next morning and invited her to lunch. She was feeling guilty about her relationship with her children – guilt seemed to be the dominant emotion in her life these days. She had always been close to her kids, especially her daughter, but since she had started gambling they saw less and less of each other. She blamed it on the fact that the kids were busy. Both kids had gone away for college which had taken an obvious toll on the time they spent together. But now, both children had moved back to Minneapolis. It was true that they worked weekdays and she worked weekends, but still she could be meeting them for lunch or inviting them over for dinner during the week. It seemed she no longer had the energy needed to maintain closeness with her family. She decided this had to change. This lunch would be the first step in renewing those relationships. After calling her daughter, she telephoned her son and made arrangements to see him the next day.

She had Stacey pick the restaurant, as she was a picky eater and was rarely satisfied with the food served. Her daughter seemed testy and put out, not at all happy to see her mother. The restaurant was a trendy Italian place. The crusty French bread was wonderful, but it was served with herbed olive oil instead of butter. Kim was glad when Stacey complained and the server brought butter to the table. The salads were delicious, although Stacey thought hers had too much dressing so the server brought her another salad with the dressing on the side. While eating her second salad, Stacey brought up the topic that was troubling her.

"I was surprised you called me today, you never seem to call anymore. You have plenty of time to run around with Pat. Guess I'm just too boring for your tastes."

"Boring? You've never bored me – you should know that. There's no one I'd rather spend my time with. And the phone works two ways you know."

"I do call," Stacey said, "You're never home."

"Why don't you leave messages? I would certainly return your calls if I knew you wanted to talk to me."

"You're my mother. I shouldn't have to leave you messages – I expect you to be home when I call."

"And to think I once doubted your paternity," Kim quipped.

"Mother, this is not a joking matter. I'm concerned about you. You've changed... I'm going to ask you a question and I want an honest answer – Mother, are you using drugs?"

Kim almost choked on her wine.

Their entrees were served. They ate in silence for a few minutes as Kim tried to think how to respond. Stacey had ordered a barbequed chicken pizza; she thought the chicken tasted odd and there was too much salt in the sauce. She tasted Kim's fettuccini; she decided she liked that much better than her lunch. She called the server to the table and complained about the pizza.

"Can we get you a different one?" the waiter asked.

"No, I'm afraid it won't be any better. Why don't you get me the fettuccini instead. Take the pizza away," Stacey said. "Oh, and get me another plate please, I'll just eat some my mother's until mine is served."

As they ate Kim's pasta, they resumed their conversation.

"No, Stacey, I am not using drugs."

"Well, something's going on with you. You're always distracted and you're nervous. You're gone all the time and when Dad's out of town, you're even gone at night. I've called you some nights until really late and you're never there." Stacey paused, looked embarrassed, and then asked, "Are you having an affair?"

"Stacey, I'm not doing anything wrong – don't worry. I'm in menopause and am having a really hard time with it. I have a lot of trouble sleeping so I have been going out more in the evenings when you're dad's gone. But you don't need to worry about that. I'm a grown woman. Pat and I just go to movies and stuff."

"You're not going to that casino, I hope. I know Pat and you used to go there. You're not developing a gambling problem are you?"

"We gamble sometimes, but I'm sure it's not a problem. It's fun but stupid. I don't plan to do it anymore. Let's just forget my recent behavior. I guess I just figured you kids were too busy for me. I'm going to go to the doctor and see if I can get on hormones or something. I'll be back to my old self in no time."

Kim was dying for a cigarette but couldn't smoke in front of her daughter. She searched in her oversized

Coach bag for a piece of gum. She found a piece of Nicorette in the bottom of her purse. A pleasant surprise, as she thought she was out. She tried to unwrap the foil backing in an unobtrusive manner so her daughter wouldn't notice. Nothing, however, had ever gotten by Stacey.

"What in the world did you just put in your mouth?" Stacey asked.

"Just a piece of gum."

"Odd wrapper. Can I have a piece?"

"Sorry," Kim said. "It was my last piece."

"What kind was it? Let me see the package."

"For heaven's sake, Stacey. Quit cross-examining me. It was just a stray piece of gum in the bottom of my purse. I don't know what kind it is, it's not very good."

Stacey ordered amaretto cheesecake for dessert, ate half of it and then sent it back.

"It tastes freezer-burned," she told the exasperated waiter.

Stacy had to get back to work so she left her mother at the restaurant. Kim ordered another drink, something she rarely did. She bought cigarettes out of a vending machine and just sat and smoked and drank while fighting back tears. She was grateful that tomorrow she'd be seeing her son rather than her daughter. Chris would not want to examine her behavior. He certainly would not accuse her of having an affair. Her son accepted her invitation because he liked to eat and figured she'd pick up the tab. Kim was sure he'd be happy with his food and not send anything back. Tomorrow would be a better day.

She stayed out of the casino for one week. She was beginning to hope that she would be able to quit gambling. She was still feeling extremely stressed and the nightmares continued, but she did believe she was regaining some control over her life. She believed that every day she didn't gamble made her stronger. She was trying to relax by taking deep breaths and using imagery when her husband called and told her that she had to go to a business dinner with him. It would not be a good night.

She dressed in her best outfit – a long, loose fitting black dress which she accessorized with her only good jewelry, a strand of pearls and matching earrings. She wore black pumps and black thigh-high hose that somehow made her feel a little wild. She thought the outfit quite stylish and flattering. Then the problems began. She had no dress coat; she had thrown it out after the visit from the police. She now wondered what had prompted her to make such a foolish, impulsive move. She attempted to get in the car without a coat but Peter stopped her.

"Where's your coat? It's freezing - you can't go out like that."

She went back inside and grabbed a jacket – Peter looked shocked.

"You can't wear that!" he exclaimed, "We're going to a fancy restaurant. I'm entertaining important people – you can't show up in a goddamn parka. Go put on your long coat."

"I gave it to charity," Kim said, feeling extremely apprehensive.

"Charity!" by now he was yelling. "Why in God's name did you do that? It's your best coat – it's your only coat."

"I thought it made me look fat," came her feeble reply.

"It's chocolate that makes you look fat. You can't blame that on a coat. If you ate the way I did, lots of fruits and vegetables, you'd look and feel better. I bet when I'm out of town, not one bit of healthy food passes through you lips. Now you're attempting to blame a coat for the way you look. Sometimes I think you're out of your mind. Okay, put that dumb jacket on. When we get to the restaurant you leave it in the car and I'll drop you at the door. I can't believe you do such stupid things."

The evening was off to a bad start and it would only get worse.

On the way home Peter said, "I've been looking at your portfolio. Your stocks are all terribly overpriced and I want you to sell them. I know I don't usually interfere with your investments but I have a lot more experience than you in these things, so I'm going to insist. Have you checked lately? Are you even aware your portfolio is worth almost $300.000?"

Kim was only too aware of the value of her portfolio: zero.

The next day Kim headed for the casino fifteen minutes after Peter left for work. She returned home, $300 poorer, ten minutes before he came home.

Where have you been all day?" he said, irritated, "I've been calling all day. I hope you sold your stocks like I told you to."

And she said the only thing she could think of, "Peter, I want a divorce."

# Chapter Nineteen

It was difficult to tell who was more shocked by Kim's request. Peter stared at her in disbelief. Kim reached in her purse and pulled out a pack of cigarettes, and, for the first time in more than twenty years, lit up in front of her husband.

"This is a joke, right?"

And Kim, continued to amaze herself by answering, "No Peter, I've given it a lot of thought, I believe it's time we divorce. The kids are grown, we have nothing in common and I think we'd both be happier apart."

"Let me get this straight," he said, "I ask you to sell some overpriced stocks, and you decide to divorce me and take up smoking."

"Told, Peter, told – you never ask – you order, I'm tired of being told what to do. I'm an adult."

"If the stocks mean so damn much to you, you can keep them. Just forget the whole thing."

But Kim didn't want to forget. She suddenly realized how badly she wanted out of the marriage. It was suddenly clear to her: she gambled because she was in a miserable marriage. Without Peter, she'd be happy. If she were happy, she wouldn't need to gamble. It was so simple. No longer would she be bossed and criticized. She would have freedom, and she wouldn't constantly be stressed because her work wasn't done, or because it wasn't done well enough to please Peter. "When was the last time he had given me a compliment," she wondered. Oh yes, she wanted out.

The thought of divorce had come to her only five minutes ago, but what she said was "Peter, I've been thinking about this for months. The stocks have nothing to do with it. True, I get upset when you issue orders, but I'm not divorcing you because of this one order. I'm divorcing you because of twenty- six years of orders."

"You better give this some serious thought, you know. You won't have the same standard of living if you divorce me."

"And what standard might that be? We never go anywhere, we eat cheap food, we scrimp on everything, and all I hear is 'save money, save money.' What the hell are we saving for? Why can't we have any fun? I don't think you even have the capacity for having a good time. You're a cheapskate and a stuffed shirt and I can provide a more enjoyable standard of living on my nurse's salary."

"How dare you call me names? I have always provided for you. Just because I'm frugal is no reason to talk about divorce. I think our marriage is just fine, and I think the way we live is the way intelligent, responsible people should live. Spending money on restaurants, fancy cars and designer clothes is stupid."

"I think you're stupid!" Kim yelled. "I think you're an idiot and a moron and I'm sick of the way we live. I'm sick of being judged and criticized, and I'm sick of being told what to do, when to do it, and how it should be done. I want to go where I want, eat what I want, live where I want, and I don't want anyone telling me what I can and can't do!"

"What did you call me?" Peter was livid.

"A stuffed shirt."

"No, no, not that. What else?"

"A cheapskate."

"No, you called me something worse. Don't you even realize what you said?"

Kim had to think. "Mmmm, let me see, oh – do you mean 'idiot and moron'?"

"Yes, I can't believe you said that. Maybe there isn't much hope for this marriage if you are going to talk to me like that!" Peter was getting more and more agitated.

"Oh for God's sake, those are such generic insults - I don't know why they upset you. Being called a stuffed shirt and a cheapskate is much worse."

"Kim, I'm not really interested in quantifying your insults. What I'm interested in is an apology, although I'm not sure I'm going to accept it."

"Don't worry about it. An apology is the last thing you're going to get out of me. I'm going out. Don't expect me home, I'm going to stay in a hotel tonight."

"What a joke, I know you're going to that damn casino. That's probably why you want a divorce; so you'll have more time to gamble."

Kim still had plenty of cash left from her winning streak a few weeks ago. The money she had won when Peter was in Paris. She had paid off the $2000 she was overdrawn but had kept the remainder of the cash stashed in a fireproof box she had hidden behind some sweaters in her closet. She planned to pay off her ready reserve. She still owed $5000, but felt embarrassed going to her bank with so many hundred-dollar bills. She thought she would pay it off in small increments; she didn't want the teller to think she was a drug dealer. She counted the bills, $6400; she took $1400, leaving enough to pay off her loan. She packed a small bag with a nightgown and toiletries, put the cash in her purse and left the house without saying another word to her husband.

When she got to the casino, she left her bag in the car thinking she would play for an hour or so then get a comped room and a good night's sleep. She, of course, never took the bag out of her car. She was in a great mood, her impulsive decision to get a divorce felt wonderful, she already felt free. Tonight she wouldn't have to worry about getting home for Peter – those days were over. She visited with total strangers, confiding in them that she had just left her husband. Several of the women she spoke with were also divorced; they were all having fun, none of them worried about going home to irate men. The machines were friendly as well, giving Kim many four-of-a-kinds. She avoided the dollar machines and played mainly fifty-cent poker. On a triple bonus poker machine she had four aces for $600. While Kim was waiting for her hand pay, the woman next to her started chatting.

"You sure are lucky tonight. Are you up or just winning back some losses?" she asked.

"Oh, I'm up," Kim said, "for a change. I can't believe how lucky I've been. I told my husband tonight that I wanted a divorce then I came here because I didn't want to stay home with him. I'm sure glad I didn't stay home, it would have been pretty grim there."

"The machines are telling you that you that you made the right decision."

"Excuse me?" Kim asked.

"The machines. They know what you've done and they react accordingly. When you've done the right thing, they reward you. When you've done the wrong thing, they punish you. It's all in your subconscious; the machines pick up your vibes.'

The last time Kim had won was during Peter's trip to France. She was quite sure she hadn't done anything during that week that deserved a reward.

The woman continued, "The machines have ESP. I come here to lose, to be punished. You see," she lowered her voice and whispered to Kim, "I've done terrible things."

"I've done terrible things, too," Kim said, "but that's when I win."

Kim wondered what had prompted her to say such a crazy thing. This woman was nuts and it was rubbing off on her. She was beginning to feel like she was at work. She was glad when the casino staff finally came with payment. She wanted to get away from this woman.

Kim played all night. After her big win she lowered her stakes. She played nickel slots and kept her bets at the minimum. She was determined to go home a winner, and she did, leaving the casino with an additional $480. She didn't want to see Peter but was sure he had already left for work. In a few days he'd be going to Europe again. She planned to avoid him until after his trip. She would have a week to think about her future without any pressure from him.

When she got home, she was surprised to see his car in the garage and even more surprised to see him sitting at the kitchen table with his head in his hands.

"We have to talk," he said.

She could not remember him ever uttering these words during the entire course of their marriage. It was always she who wanted to talk and Peter who refused. She now realized how irritating these words could be.

"Have you come to your senses, yet," he asked.

"I came to my senses when I asked for a divorce."

"So you're bound and determined to do this? You know I'm going out of town again, perhaps you'd like to think about it while I'm gone."

"Peter, it's the right thing, the divorce. It's what I need to do."

"You couldn't have had worse timing, with my trip and everything."

"There would never be a good time."

"Money," Peter said. "What about money?"

"What about money?"

"Have you thought about a financial settlement? How do you want to divide things? If we sell all our investments, we'll have a lot of capital gains to pay. Do you just want us to keep our own portfolios and call it even? And another thing - I plan to stay in this house, I picked it out, I paid for it and I love it – just because you've lost your mind doesn't mean my whole life should be turned upside down. And you've got a job now, so I hope you don't expect any alimony. You make plenty to support yourself."

"Are you saying that I get my portfolio and nothing else? You can stay in the house but you have to give me half the value. And your 401K, what about that? Yours is worth a lot more than mine. These things all have to be divided equally."

Peter said he had taken the day off and was going to spend the afternoon in their home office working on an equitable settlement. He did not want to be disturbed.

Four hours later Peter emerged from their office area carrying two tax books, a large manila envelope, and several charts and graphs. Kim knew that whatever number Peter had come up with, this was the settlement she would receive. She could not argue math with Peter, in this area he had all the advantages. She could, of course, hire an attorney, but knowing Peter, this would be a disaster. He would fight her to the death, till every last penny they had was gone. He could be that obstinate when challenged. Plus, she worried if they got into a legal battle, that her actual financial situation would be revealed. That was still her greatest fear; she could not bear for Peter and her children to know how stupid she had been.

"Spreadsheets or bar graphs? I made up both." Peter asked as he held up some charts showing Kim's nonexistent assets and his very real ones.

"I don't need to see either; I just want to know the bottom line."

"It will take some explanation," Peter said. "You can't just determine assets. You have to look at tax laws, capital gains, and penalties that may have to be paid if they were sold. You also have to look at the expenses that I'll incur when I sell this house. They have to be taken off its value. After all, if we sold the house those costs would cut into the profits."

"How much, Peter? How much are you going to give me?"

"$150,000 – I think that's very fair. You will also get to keep your car and personal belongings. I will keep the household furnishings."

Furniture was a topic Kim felt competent to argue. After some angry discussion, Peter agreed to let her keep her bedroom set, the kitchen table, a small TV and a recliner.

Peter had always told her they were millionaires. Every time she complained about his tightwad ways, he would say, "That's why I'm a millionaire."

So why was she was only getting $150,000?

Of course, there was the $300,000 portfolio of Internet stocks which Peter had taken into account when determining the settlement. If, in fact, that actually existed, she would be walking away from the marriage with a healthy $450,000. She also had around $40,000 in her 401K so Peter actually believed she had a total net worth of $490,000. He was also unaware of her ballooning credit card debt that now exceeded $32,000. Based on the facts as he knew them he had made a relatively fair division of assets, and Kim was too embarrassed to set him straight.

Kim tried to look on the bright side. After the divorce she'd be able to pay off all her debts and still have enough to buy a small townhouse. She made a decent salary and she'd still have her 401K. She'd be fine.

Two days later they met with an attorney. They had agreed one attorney could handle the divorce as they had arranged a settlement on their own.

"I don't see any problem with what you two have worked out. You both have good jobs and you've divided your property quite fairly. Since there are no minor children involved, you shouldn't even have to appear in court. I'll get the paperwork started; you should receive a decision in a couple of months."

"What do you mean by decision?" Kim asked the lawyer.

"I mean, your divorce should be final in two months."

'Twenty-six years,' Kim thought, 'and in two months, it will all be over."

The following day Peter went to Europe and Kim found an apartment. She thought finding a place to stay would be difficult. She knew the rental market was tight and that people often looked for months before being accepted for appropriate housing. But she was an employed, single, middle-aged woman with no children or pets, and she was able to pay her first and last month's rent plus the damage deposit – she was a landlord's dream. She rented the third place she looked at;

it was small, an efficiency apartment, which was basically only one room and a bath. But it was clean, reasonable, and in a nice area. It was located only twelve miles from the casino, but she told herself that the close proximity to Jackpot Casino would not encourage her to gamble – those days were behind her. The apartment was vacant and she could move in the next day.

She now had the most difficult job of all: telling her children she was getting a divorce. She fixed herself a drink, an uncommon occurrence, but Kim was desperate for any courage she could muster, even if it came from a vodka bottle. She sipped her Bloody Mary and puffed on a cigarette trying to think of a gentle way to break the news. She wanted her children to know that the divorce would be amiable and that they still could be considered a family. She knew better than to criticize her husband to their children. This was to be a congenial, even pleasant divorce. As she tried to come up with the right words the phone rang. It was Stacy.

"I talked with Dad. He said you're getting a divorce. I can't believe it. You two have been married over twenty years. Mother, I think you're losing your mind."

"Stacy, your dad and I have nothing in common. It will be a friendly divorce; we just both feel we'd be happier apart. It's not like we're mad at each other or anything. We've just grown apart."

"He said you called him an idiot and a moron."

"Oh for God's sake – I called him a lot worse than that, he's just too stupid to have noticed."

"Mother! Dad is not stupid – he has a PhD."

"Big deal. There's more to life than calculus, and when it comes to people skills, your father is an ignoramus. I'm sick of him and his bossiness and his frigging superiority. I'm tired of waiting on him, picking up after him, washing his laundry, and being his slave."

"I thought this was going to be a friendly divorce," Stacy said. "Right now your 'people skills' don't sound much better than his."

"Whose side are you on, Stacy? I thought you'd understand."

"Well, I don't understand, and I'm not taking sides. I know Dad is difficult, but after all these years, it seems you should be used to him"

"I'm sorry; I don't mean to put you in the middle. I've just been so unhappy. I don't want this to come between us."

They spoke for a long time, Kim trying to make her daughter understand without being too critical of her husband. He was, after all, Stacy's father and she knew Stacy loved him. By the time they hung up, things were quite warm between the two women, Stacy had finally acknowledged that Kim's marriage had been difficult, and she wished her mother the best. She even agreed to help Kim move into her new apartment tomorrow.

"I'll call Chris," Stacy volunteered. "He'll probably help too. We could use a little muscle on this job."

Kim fixed herself another drink, hoping for once she could get drunk before she got a hangover. Usually just as she was feeling the effects of the liquor, her headache would begin. This intolerance to alcohol was probably a blessing considering her addictive personality. As she was debating adding Tabasco to her drink, the phone rang again.

"Mother," it was Chris.

Kim took a long swallow from her drink.

"I've spoken to Stacy and Dad. I don't know what to say."

That didn't surprise Kim, but it did relieve her. She wasn't up to another emotional conversation like she had just had with Stacy.

"Mom, are you okay? Dad says he thinks you're cracking up. He said you called him names, he said you called him a ..."

Kim interrupted, "Let's not even go there. I just said some things in the heat of the moment, it didn't mean anything," she said.

Chris, like his father, disliked talking about anything of a personal nature. After a couple of feeble attempts to offer his mother support, he was grateful to quit discussing the emotional aspects of divorce and concentrate of the logistics of Kim's move. He agreed to help her pack up her things and move to the new apartment tomorrow.

As she hung up the phone, she felt the beginning of the headache. "Not even a buzz from these drinks," she thought. "Nothing but a hangover. Shit - I had really wanted to get loaded."

The following night after her children had left and her apartment was in order, Kim surveyed her new home. For the past fourteen years, she had lived in a 2600 square foot house on a two-acre lot; she now lived in a bedroom that had a kitchen on one wall. She looked at the small stove and refrigerator and decided "kitchen" was too grandiose a term. "Kitchenette," she thought, "I'll call it a kitchenette." She reminded herself that this was only temporary; once she was divorced she'd buy a decent place of her own. She could get by till then. The last few days had been exhausting and she was sure tonight she would fall asleep as soon as her head hit the pillow.

She did fall asleep, almost immediately, but was awakened in the middle of the night by dreams - deeply disturbing dreams. Cockroaches... In her sleep she had imagined her new apartment was crawling with them and that she was shooting them with a tiny gun that fit easily into the palm of her hand - a gun that seemed, somehow, familiar to her. She had deadly aim during this nightmare; she was able to pick off the roaches easily by shooting them in their microscopic foreheads, right above and between their eyes.

She awoke with a start, turned on the light and then panicked. What if there were bugs? She didn't want to see them. She turned off the light. But cockroaches would stay out in the dark; they would run if she turned on the light. She needed the light on but was afraid she would see them scurrying for cover once the room was illuminated. She lay there trying to decide what to do. Finally she closed her eyes, fumbled in the dark for the light switch and remained still with her eyes closed for five minutes – enough time for the bugs to disappear.

Nothing was amiss when she opened her eyes. She was dying for a cigarette but had none. She sat up in bed, feeling terrified, feeling crazy. She knew there were no cockroaches, but she was afraid of them anyway. She knew she wouldn't be able to remain in the apartment all night.

She needed to make herself at home during the day; the nighttime was just too scary. She opened one of the three doors in her apartment, the one to her closet, and took out a long knit dress. Kim slipped it on, put on her shoes, grabbed her purse and keys and ran out the door. She hadn't even bothered to comb her hair. "I'll return after daylight," she thought. It was three A.M., there was only one place she could go at that hour; she headed for the casino.

# Chapter Twenty

Two months later, Kim's divorce was official. "It must be a record," she thought. Friends at work had been separated months, sometimes years, before their divorces were finalized. Eight and a half weeks after she moved into her efficiency apartment, she took in her mail and there it was - the divorce decree. Peter now had seven days in which to give her the $150,000 settlement he owed her and, knowing Peter, she would not receive it one day early. He would want to squeeze every last cent of interest out of that money.

She telephoned him to make arrangements to receive payment and, as expected, he told her to come over to his house in one week and he would give her a check. She had not been able to quit gambling since separating from her husband, and her credit card debt had continued to climb during that time. In one week though, she'd be able to pay off what she owed, and she was determined then to quit for good.

She wanted to find a condo or townhouse. She now would have less than $100,000 to spend, but thought she could find something in that range and if need be she was willing to take out a small mortgage. In one week her gambling would be behind her and she'd be on the road to recovery. She would be out of debt and soon would be in a place of her own. It sounded great. She headed for the casino as she did most nights. She felt relieved that she had only seven more days of this foolishness.

She really believed this time she would quit. Kim had one week to get that place out of her system. "Quitting shouldn't be hard," she thought. After all, she had come to hate going there. Sometimes she would feel so tired, and her little apartment would seem so warm and cozy and all she would really want to do was curl up in bed with a good book, yet, she would find herself driving to the casino, her mood darkening, feeling angry and out of control. She never understood the compulsion that forced her back there night after night, knowing she would only lose money and return home depressed. But now she had a date when the craziness would end. One week. In seven days she would be free. She felt good driving there tonight, sort of like she was about to give notice at a job she hated. She was almost expecting a going away party; she was such a regular at the place.

Kim decided to try something new in an attempt to leave the place a winner. The machines gobbled twenty-dollar bills up in no time. She thought her money might last longer if she played with tens instead. If a machine was cold, she would quit after losing ten rather than twenty, as she rarely took coins out but just played till her credits were gone. She decided to take out a thousand dollar cash advance on her credit card. She didn't plan to spend it all that night: she was hoping to spread it out till the end of the week when she was going to quit gambling. When she finally got to the front of the line at the cashier's cage, she requested her money in ten-dollar bills. The cashier glared at her.

"You want a thousand bucks in tens? You gotta be kidding!"

"Yes, please. I think my money might last longer in smaller bills."

"Maybe you'd like it in ones," the annoyed cashier answered, "then you could stay here all year."

Kim felt her temper flare. With all the money she'd lost in this place, they could at least treat her with respect.

"Ones would be silly," Kim said. "I'll take it in fives."

"Fives! Have you looked behind you? There's a long line of people waiting. I can't take the time to count out one thousand dollars in five-dollar bills."

"If you didn't waste so much time with sarcasm and complaining, you could have already given me my money. I want it in fives and if you're not willing to cooperate I'd like to speak with your supervisor."

The five-dollar bills made a huge pile. Kim felt rich. Had she gotten it in hundreds, as she often did, she would have been able to tuck the bills into her wallet without them even making a bulge. This was much more satisfying. The bills wouldn't even fit in the zipper compartment of her Coach bag; they overflowed into the main compartment where they were at risk of being permanently lost, as this purse was enormous and tended to attract more trash than most garbage cans. She went into the bathroom and while sitting on the toilet, attempted to organize the voluminous amount of money. She had seven days left to gamble. She attempted to divide 1000 by seven, hmmm.... not easy, she knew it had to be around $140 a day. She divided her money into seven piles each containing twenty-eight fives. She had twenty dollars left, which she tucked into her large black zip-around wallet. She took out one pile and inserted it into the zipper compartment of her purse and the remainder she dropped into the large black void of her handbag. She assured herself she would not gamble with any more than tonight's allotment.

She scanned the casino in the hope that some machine would signal her to play. Her friend Liz was extraordinarily lucky; she always claimed she could read the machines and that they communicated to her a willingness to pay. Kim received no vibes and no signals; the machines remained inanimate money grubbers. If they gave out any message, it was "c'mon sucker". She turned her attention to the gamblers, looking for banks of players that looked happy, players who looked like winners. No such animal seemed to exist. She started looking instead for big losers, in the hopes they would leave their machines just as they were due to warm up. Losers were easier to find. She soon sat down at a machine that was vacated by an angry man who claimed to have sunk over $200 in it.

"Not a damn thing," he grumbled. "Two hundred bucks and not even one four-of-a-kind."

He lumbered off, leaving in his wake the smell of body odor and stale smoke. He had been playing with coins rather than bills and the machine was littered with coin wrappers. The screen of the poker machine was covered with ashes. Kim gathered up the paper and threw it in a large trashcan sitting next to the end machine. She blew the ashes off the screen and began to play. She slid a five into the bill collector, hit the max play button, and watched as her money disappeared in the blink of an eye. It must be due to hit, she thought. She slid in two fives and they too, were soon gobbled up. She again fed the bill collector, this time using four of her bills, thinking fives were a pain. She wished she had gotten her money in twenties. Within an hour her nightly cash allotment was gone. Kim decided to move to the adjoining machine and for money she dipped into the next night's stash.

Right after she moved, a young fellow who had been sitting three seats down from Kim got up and moved to the machine she had just left.

"I've been playing this bank for hours," he said. "This machine has been played nonstop; it must be due to loosen up. These things go in cycles, you know."

He soon hit four aces, a $200 win on double bonus poker. Kim did not congratulate him - just cashed out the remaining ten quarters she had left in her machine and walked away. She tried not to feel angry. "Timing," she told herself, "it's all timing. I wouldn't have gotten that." But despite her self-talk, she was livid and believed the aces should have been hers. She vaguely remembered a woman telling her she had put just five dollars in a dollar poker machine and had been dealt a Royal Flush. Kim was unable to remember the details of that conversation, but she did remember the woman's statement quite clearly.

She hiked over to her favorite bank of dollar machines, and inserted five dollars into the end machine. She was dealt a pair of deuces. Four deuces would be nice, she thought. She threw the other three cards and was dealt another small pair. She got her bet back. She continued to play this machine, tediously inserting her remaining five dollar bills. Each bill was only one hand, and the pile of money in her purse soon disappeared.

Her mood was dark, and she was angry at the casino, angry with herself, and angry with anyone who dared to win. She knew she should go home - when she felt this way, desperate and out of control, she always lost. She again swiped her credit card through the machine next to the main cashier's cage and punched in $1000. The machine informed her of a $55.95 charge.

It asked her if she wanted to proceed. "Fucking right," she thought. She hit the "yes" button and proceeded to the cage. The next available cashier was the same snotty woman who had last waited on her.

The cashier smiled sweetly at Kim, "And how would you like that, dear? Perhaps in rolls of nickels?"

Kim chewed on her lower lip, forced herself to count to ten, and answered, "Large bills, please."

She returned to the poker machines. She slid in a hundred dollar bill and began to play. Her luck finally improved, which was a good thing as she only had $200 remaining. She hit four threes for $400. She cashed out. Dollar tokens filled the bin, and she scooped them into a large cup. As she was tossing in the tokens, she heard one drop on the floor. She reached down to get it but it had rolled behind the large wastebasket. The trash container was too heavy to move, so she had to bend over and stretch to reach the corner where the coin had lodged.

As she bent over double and extended her arm, she heard the sound of cloth tearing; the sound that sends fear into the heart of every woman who has worn a pair of pants that was a size too small. She tried to remember what underpants she was wearing and was dismayed when she remembered she was wearing her favorite – seamless, sheer, flesh–colored panties. Any- one standing behind her would be sure to think she was mooning him. "The hell with it," she thought, stretched a little further and was able to grasp the coin. Another ripping sound was heard. She stood up with the dollar in her hand. She dropped it into the bucket then self- consciously pulled her long top down over the seat of her pants.

She gathered up her pails of money and proceeded to the cashier. She walked erectly, tucking in her but- tocks in the hope that her top would hang long and loose, covering up the split seam. She continued to play, occasionally being rewarded with a four-of-a-kind, and more often punished by the sound of her pants disintegrating. Seven hours later she was again out of money. She went home, no longer caring about her pants, hearing the seam give with every movement. Once she got home she slipped off the pants and threw them in the garbage. She then summoned up her courage to face her enemy – the bed. She knew she would toss and turn and worry about money. She knew she would cough and her head would ache. She knew she would finally sleep only to be awakened by nightmares. "What a loser," Kim thought. She began to cry.

When sleep finally came, it was especially tortured. The fragments of the visions that had been disturbing her for months cohered and formed a complete and terrifying tale of thievery and murder. In the dream, she was in the casino parking lot, she had a gun, and she shot a woman and took her money. She awoke with a start and with a sense of déjà vu. This was no dream. This was familiar and far too real, and it remained real even as she totally awakened. Kim felt herself tremble and her head felt ready to explode. It was the woman, she was dreaming about the woman – the woman killed while Kim was playing at the casino. Kim was the murderer. "No," she thought, "I couldn't have done it; my mind is playing tricks on me, just like it does to my patients." Her stomach churned. She was able to reach her toilet before throwing up. That was the only luck she had had in a long time.

# Chapter Twenty-One

In the morning she made an appointment with a psychiatrist. She began to sob when she called her clinic's nurse hotline and asked for a referral. The woman that helped her was probably more comfortable with chest pain than tears. She made an appointment for Kim the same day. The woman sounded upset by Kim, which upset Kim further.

"Look, I'm not standing on a ledge or anything. I don't need to see someone today. I can wait for an appointment - this isn't an emergency or anything," Kim broke down and was barely able to form words. As she gasped for air, she added, "I don't even know if I need help."

The woman paused, obviously trying to find the right words, "Are you thinking of … m-m-m-m… hurting yourself?"

"I hurt myself everyday," Kim whispered.

At the doctor's office she was first interviewed by a nurse who took a lengthy, albeit, incomplete history. Kim said she wanted to be seen for insomnia. She finally agreed she may be having some symptoms of depression. Gambling was never mentioned. Kim was aware that she was giving a skewed explanation of her problems. She sounded like someone suffering from a mild case of depression or grief secondary to the dissolution of a long-term marriage. The nurse left the room. Kim sat there fidgeting nervously until the doctor appeared. He introduced himself then sat down, adjusted his glasses and began to read his nurse's notes. He seemed to read forever without speaking. Kim sat there expectantly. Her lips formed an exaggerated, incongruous smile and she began to prattle nervously about the weather, in a voice that sounded foreign to her – high pitched and childlike. She couldn't believe this; she worked with psychiatrists all the time, why was this one making her so uncomfortable? "He must not be any good," she thought. Her lips remained in their distinct u shape even as she spoke. She felt her eyes well with tears and tried to open them wider in an attempt to staunch the tears and look cheerful. "Psycho broad," she thought.

Finally he looked up from his papers and acknowledged her presence. He watched her for a long time. Her lips appeared to be in rictus, her eyes got rounder and her cheeks got wetter.

"Is that how you smile?" he asked.

"Yes," came the squeaky reply.

"You have tears rolling down your cheeks."

He pushed a box of Kleenex next to her and suggested, "Perhaps you should just let your face do what comes naturally. That smile seems a tad bit forced."

She gratefully took a Kleenex along with his advice and felt her face crumple. The tears now flowed unchecked and she put her face in her hands.

"I smoke," she said in a soft, low, almost inaudible voice.

He said nothing.

"And I gamble," she whispered.

"I see."

113

"I don't think it's a really big problem," Kim said, "but I have lost a lot of money and I think I'm beginning to have delusions."

"Delusions? What kind of delusions?"

"Well, they're not really delusions. They're more like bad dreams. I dream bad things have happened at the casino, and when I wake up, it seems these things are real."

"What kinds of 'bad things' happen?"

"Um, a woman was killed there. It happened while I was there and I dream that I killed her. Sometimes I see glimpses of her car, like a flashback. When I woke up today it seemed like I had really killed her."

"And, did you?"

Kim was shocked, "Of course not. I'm a nurse. I help people. I would never hurt anyone."

"Then why do you think you dream you're a murderer?"

"Guilt. Guilt I suppose, I have tremendous guilt over gambling."

"Did gambling play a part in your divorce? I see you had been married a long time."

"Yes, I divorced my husband to keep him from learning how much I had lost."

"And how much have you lost?" he asked.

"I don't really know, maybe a hundred thousand, probably more. I don't like to think about it. I've never kept any records. All I know is that all my savings and every cent I've earned for the past few years have been lost at that place."

"And your husband never knew? How did you manage to keep it from him?"

"I had bought quite a few stocks before I started gambling. I sold them to pay gambling debts, and then pretended to buy other stocks. It got pretty complicated. The bottom line is I lost everything, and even

114

worse, the stocks I pretended to buy did really well so my husband, I mean ex-husband, thinks I've got lots of money."

"Have you thought about going into treatment for your problem?"

"I absolutely refuse anything that's inpatient. I work in a hospital psych unit. I couldn't bear to be a patient in one."

Finally she and her doctor agreed on a treatment plan. Kim was to cease gambling immediately, she was to join Gamblers Anonymous, and she was to start on Prozac, a medication for depression and compulsive disorders. She was to see him again in one week.

Kim felt a flutter of optimism as she drove from the doctor's office to the pharmacy. She had little faith in G.A. and she had no faith in herself, but she had great faith in medication. After all, giving meds was her stock and trade. She was eager to start her Prozac and swallowed one dry as soon as she got her prescription filled.

# Chapter Twenty-Two

The pills didn't help; instead they made her feel worse. She was restless all the time; at night in bed she couldn't keep her legs still. The desire to gamble did not abate and she would find herself getting out of bed and going to the casino just to keep her mind off the side effects she was experiencing. A fine rash began to develop on her body and she wondered if she was allergic to the medication. Kim kept swallowing the pills though, in the hope that eventually they would kick in and she would be cured. Her settlement from Peter was rapidly disappearing. She felt sick, anxious, out of control, and unbearably depressed. The dreams continued. She was now smoking three packs of cigarettes a day. She no longer bothered with patches or gum, but was simply giving into her addictions. Tomorrow was Saturday; she didn't know if she would be able to make it to work, she felt so terrible.

The alarm rang at 5 A.M. Kim had slept only two hours. Her head ached, her jaw was clenched, and her feet were dancing to their own private drummer. "Damn medication," she thought. She forced herself out of bed. She didn't dare call in sick. She was a single woman now and she couldn't jeopardize her job.

She sat down to report at seven. The unit was quiet with most of the patients still asleep. An admission was on its way which Kim volunteered to take. Usually the nurses took turns doing admissions, and Kim just wanted to get hers out of the way.

The admission was a young woman named Elizabeth who had been found by store security at Dayton's, a large department store in downtown Minneapolis. She was found hiding in a dressing room in the middle of the night. The police were called and she was brought to the hospital after telling the police why she was hiding in the store.

"Call me Beth," the young woman requested after Kim introduced herself.

"Beth, I know you were hiding in Dayton's, can you tell me why?" Kim asked.

"I have OCD, Obsessive Compulsive Disorder, and there are certain things I have to do. For example, when I brush my teeth I have to do it seventeen times in a row, one minute each time - that's why I don't brush my teeth very often. Everything's like that, there's a rule for everything I do, and I can't break the rules without feeling sick. Yesterday I made a terrible mistake - you see, I always have to exit any place the same way I entered. You know, use the same door, the same elevator, stuff like that. Well, I wasn't thinking and I used the 'up' escalator at Dayton's. I was trapped on the second floor. I couldn't run down the 'up' escalator because there were always people on it. Plus I have a problem with my gait and I'm not able to run at all"

"I see you use a cane," Kim said, "What's the matter with your leg?"

"Well, there's nothing really wrong with it. It's just that I always have to lead with my left foot because I can't let my right foot get in front on my left foot – so when I walk it looks pretty weird. I use a cane and act like my leg is lame so people won't think I'm crazy. I can only go up one step at a time, so you see, I could never have run the wrong way on a moving escalator."

"Okay," Kim said, "you were stuck on the second floor, then what happened?"

"I remained there until the store closed. I hid in a dressing room; I might have remained there all night except I was so nervous I lit up a cigarette to help me calm down. I guess the smoke alerted Security. Anyway, they called the police and they came and took me here, which has caused another problem. They took me out a different door. Now I'll have to go back and fix it."

"And how do you do that?" Kim asked.

"Well, I'll have to try to retrace my steps. I'll enter through the door they took me out of, then exit through the door I entered yesterday. It gets pretty confusing and fixing things is never as good as doing them right in the first place. I know I'll be a nervous wreck until it gets fixed," she paused then said, "I'm not stupid you know. I'm aware my behavior is crazy and I know it's wrecking my life but I'm powerless to change. I'm sure a normal person like you can't understand it."

"I understand better than you think," Kim said softly.

The two women sat together quietly, each contemplating her private hell.

Then Beth added, "The worst thing is that I know I'll never get better. I've seen a zillion psychiatrists and tried every medication. The doctors have no answers other than meds, and the meds don't help. They just give me side effects and make me feel worse. Nothing can help compulsive disorders."

Kim looked around her at all the patients who were in the dayroom. They would never be really cured. Even when doing well, they were still at risk for a relapse. The ones who were control were the ones that were so medicated they looked like zombies, shuffling about the unit, stiff and uncomfortable; their faces expressionless masks, their lives even more empty now than when they were in the throes of their illnesses. When Kim went home that night, she threw her Prozac in the garbage.

# Chapter Twenty-Three

She was awakened from her restless sleep by the phone ringing. It was Stacy, "Mother, where have you been? I call all the time and you're never home. I was afraid you were dead or something. I called Dad."

Kim felt her anxiety level increase, "And what did he have to say?"

"He said you have a gambling problem. He didn't want to tell me but I was beside myself. He said you were probably at the casino. Is it true?"

"I wouldn't call it a problem." was Kim's feeble reply.

"You're gone day and night, and you never call me! It's like I don't exist for you anymore. I'd call that a problem. Dad says that's the real reason you divorced him, so you'd have more time to gamble."

"Your dad just doesn't want to look at his own behavior."

"And it seems," Stacy said, "that you don't want to look at yours either."

"I just like to have a little fun now and then," Kim said.

"A little fun?" Stacy was yelling. "A little fun? You've divorced your husband and abandoned your children! I've called your friends looking for you and it seems you've dumped them as well. You need help, you're sick!" Stacy calmed down, then added quietly, "Mother, is there something I can do to help you quit gambling?"

Kim again reiterated, "It's not a problem. I just like to have a little fun."

Stacy's voice became menacing, "Well, don't think I'll be here for you when you've lost everything. Neither my brother nor I will help you unless you're willing to quit gambling right now. We've talked it over, and if you care about us you have to quit this insanity right now. We're giving you a choice: your children or that damn casino."

"I just like to have a little fun…"

"Good-bye Mother."

The phone went dead.

Kim couldn't believe it; her children couldn't just drop her. She realized, with guilt, that she had ignored her kids since she had started gambling. She pretty much ignored everyone now, just spent all her time at Jackpot Casino alone, because that's how she preferred to gamble. She thought about calling Stacy back to try to make up with her, maybe invite her out to dinner tonight. She hated having her children angry with her. She decided to give Stacy a chance to cool off. She'd call her tomorrow. Kim got dressed and headed for the bank.

She had now been divorced three months. She had gambled almost every day. She was averaging about $1000 a day in losses and her money from Peter was almost gone. She realized she had given up and that she no longer thought about quitting gambling. She now thought only about ways to obtain money to feed

121

her addiction. Kim believed the only thing that could make her quit would be a big win, a win large enough to make up for all that she had lost, a win that would allow her to start over. If she could win her money back, she would be able to buy a townhouse and pay off her credit cards. She could prove to her children that she didn't have a problem, and they could all start being close again. The problem was the stakes she played. The most she could win on dollar video poker was $4000 for a Royal Flush, and they were few and far between. Plus, $4000 was a drop in the bucket compared to all she had lost. She needed higher stakes in order to be once again made whole. She withdrew her remaining balance from her checking account, $10,000; she received it in $100 bills. She decided she would play $25 video poker. That worked out to $125 a hand. It was a lot to gamble, but one winning streak and she could win her losses back. Playing at those high stakes meant she would win $20,000 for four aces and $100,000 for a Royal. All she needed was one winning streak.

She slid two bills into the bill collector and hit the draw button. She slid in five more bills after losing the first hand. She sat there feeding the machine and selecting cards to hold. In exactly forty-nine minutes her money was gone. Ten thousand dollars lost in less than an hour. Her divorce settlement was history, and she owed a lot on her credit cards. For the first time in her adult life she knew what it meant to be destitute. She lit up a cigarette, inhaled deeply and thought about what she should do. She felt someone watching her. She turned around - Stacey was standing behind her.

"It's true, isn't it? I came here to see for myself. I felt so bad about the things I said, but it's all true." Stacey was crying. She turned and walked away.

Kim called after her, "Wait, it's not what you think, how long have you been here?"

But Stacey didn't answer, didn't even turn around, she just headed toward the exit. Kim watched her daughter's back as it disappeared from view.

A familiar gnawing feeling formed in Kim's gut. She gobbled down a couple of Maalox tablets and felt immediate relief. She swallowed a couple of Motrin with her Diet Coke and tried to put Stacey out of her mind. Gambling would make her forget anything. She could still cash a check; she had her ready reserve available. That had been paid off when she first got her settlement. She wrote a check for $1000 and lowered her bets to $5.00 poker. She soon lost that thousand as well. She had only played for a couple of hours and she was down $11,000. She knew she should go home, but dreaded the idea because she knew she would ruminate about her fight with her daughter and knew she'd be unable to sleep tonight because of nightmares. The more she lost, the worse the dreams. She wrote another $1000 check and returned to her old favorites, the dollar poker machines. Her luck improved. She played all day and late into the night. By four in the morning, she was broke and decided to go home.

Once she was home, the enormity of what she had done sunk in – she had just lost $12,000. She had wasted her entire divorce settlement. She was overdrawn and she had large balances on her credit cards from her numerous cash advances. Her paycheck was barely enough to cover all her minimum payments and her living expenses. She would be in debt forever, there was no money left with which to gamble. And her children... what must they think of her? She thought of the expression on Stacey's face - she had looked disgusted. She knew her children took after their father in many ways. Like him, they could be quite rigid and unforgiving. Would they ever want her back in their lives, or was it too late? Had she lost even more than money?

She continued to gamble that week using her credit cards until they all reached their maximums and the casino refused to give her any more money. That weekend at work she felt like someone going through withdrawal. She was in a panic, having no way to get her hands on money with which to play. Kim had destroyed her family and alienated her friends, but she did pride herself on her job. She always did her best at work. But this weekend that was all about to change. She had to get money to feed her addiction, and she was willing to break her patients' trust in order to that. In the med room was a locked box that contained all the money patients had brought into the hospital with them. Most of them had little money, but there were forty patients. The small sums added up. Kim donned a pair of disposable gloves and when all the other staff seemed busy; she went into the med room and unlocked the box. She quickly went through the envelopes, sliding the bills out and slipping them into her pocket. She was quite intent on her task and was unaware when another nurse quietly entered the room. By the time she had finished her task, the other nurse was gone and Kim was unaware she had been observed. That night as she was leaving the hospital she was stopped by Security, they brought her back to the unit where her boss, who had been notified at home, was waiting.

"I don't know what possible explanation you might have, but I guess I have to ask. Is there any legitimate reason for you to have taken all the patients' money?" he asked.

"I have a gambling problem," Kim answered.

"I'm sorry you've sunk so low, Kim, but I'm going to have to terminate your employment here immediately. I will also have to notify the nursing board. I don't think you should plan to work again as a nurse. I will not contact the police and press charges unless the hospital insists, it seems to me you're being punished enough."

Kim was shocked, "I'm fired, no ... what about treatment? When Sandy stole that credit card you sent her to treatment. Shouldn't I be treated the same."

"Sandy stole from a credit card company, you stole from patients, from people who have so little, who are entrusted to you for their care. That's a much greater crime in my book. I can't treat this lightly, Kim. You no longer have a job with this hospital. Your last paycheck will be mailed to your home. If you have any belongings here I suggest you get them now. You will not be allowed back on this unit."

Kim emptied her locker of its contents. All traces of her were now removed from the hospital except for the gossip that her sudden absence would generate. Oh yes, she would provide great fuel for the gossip mill. There would be no going-away party, no cards, and no gifts. Her career was over.

During the next few days, Kim thought she was losing her mind. She worried nonstop about money. How would she live? She didn't dare contact her family; they were all sick of her. There was no longer anyone who cared about her. She wrote checks at the casino, knowing she was exceeding her ready reserve, hoping her final paycheck would cover the checks she was writing. She contacted the Benefits department at work and completed the necessary forms to withdraw her 401K money. Her rent was due, but she didn't bother to pay it.

Her final check and the retirement money provided her again with playing money, but it didn't last long. She made no attempt to pay any bills, as she needed every cent in her checking account for gambling. When she received an eviction notice from her landlord, she ignored it.

She continued to gamble daily, trying to limit herself, trying to make the money last. One day when she returned from the casino her possessions were all laying on the front yard and her key no longer worked in her apartment's lock. She packed her car with as many of her belongings as would fit. She returned to the casino.

She stayed there for two days, writing checks she knew would bounce. She swiped her ATM card through the machine and received the message "insufficient funds." She attempted to get her check writing privileges increased. She was sent to the check services department where they told her that her check writing privileges were now suspended as her bank had returned one of her checks. She returned to the cashier's cage and attempted to get another cash advance on one of her credit cards but her requests were all denied.

She walked away from the cashier's cage, feeling deflated, empty, and lost. She scrounged in her purse looking for cigarettes and money. She was out of smokes but did find three quarters and scanned the area for a machine to play. A miracle, she needed a miracle. She spotted a twenty-five cent "red, white and blue" slot and sat down at it. Max play was three coins. She slid her last three quarters into the slot and prayed.

She lost.

She continued to sit at the machine, her mind almost blank and her face expressionless. She looked straight ahead but saw nothing. In her trance-like state, her mind began to wander, to go back to her youth, to the poetry she had loved as a teenager. She had preferred dark, brooding, fatalistic poems and one of her favorites now began echoing in her brain,

*"This is the way the world ends,*
*This is the way the world ends,"*

Tears streamed down her cheeks.

*"This is the way the world ends,*
*Not with a bang but a whimper."*

She didn't know how long she sat there, silently weeping, immersed in her own depression and T.S. Elliott's words.

*"This is the way the world ends."*

"Excuse me, ma'am," her thoughts were interrupted by a security guard. "The machines are for players only, and someone would like to play here. You're at her 'lucky machine'. I'm going to have to ask you to move."

Kim got up and walked to the exit, as she had no other options. She located her car, slid in and started the ignition. She sat there until someone honked at her; he wanted her parking space. She drove out of the parking lot, but when she got to the road she didn't know which direction to turn, for she had no place left to go.

## The End